SACRED PREY

SACRED PREY

VIVIAN SCHILLING

TRUMAN
PRESS

Published by Truman Press
15445 Ventura Boulevard
Sherman Oaks, CA 91403

Library of Congress Catalog Card Number
93-60833
ISBN 0-9637846-0-9

Printed in the United States of America
First Edition
Second printing

To the memory of my parents,
Don and Lou,
for the enchanting ride of life.

ACKNOWLEDGMENTS

*With much gratitude and affection I would like to thank
Eric Parkinson for his unyielding support throughout the years.*

*Many thanks to my editor, Shari Lovendahl; and to my reading
committee: Tom Horton, Cathy Armstrong, Janet Cummins, and Charlie Shepard;
and to my dear friend, Gina Korsi.*

*With special thanks to the City of New Orleans
for their gracious hospitality.*

SACRED PREY

Chapter 1

The bayou moaned in the darkness like a vast creature hungry for life to feed the voices of its dead. A dirt road, illuminated by bright moonlight, cut through the black swamp of southern Louisiana. It was completely still, except for the night sounds of the wooded area.

A low rumble began in the distance. Then, like a flash, a Pontiac sped past, leaving a tremendous dust cloud in its wake. Particles of clay clung to the humid air muffling the whine of the disappearing car. Just as the sound subsided, a rattling old Ford raced by in pursuit. Moments later, the headlights of a sleek Lincoln Continental cut through the increasingly thick dust cloud created by the two previous cars.

Adam Claiborne, seated on the passenger side of the Lincoln, stared intently ahead, trying desperately to see the tail-lights of the car in front of him. As he was carried deeper and deeper into the dense swamp, he felt a weight bearing down on his chest. He loosened his silk tie but it was still impossible to breathe. The dust was becoming unbearable. His green eyes narrowed and then began to tear.

"Jesus," he mumbled.

He looked over at his brother, Kyle, who excitedly steered the car. The speedometer light shone up from the dashboard giving Kyle's long, rugged features a distorted appearance.

Adam noticed that the chilling malevolence had returned to his brother's eyes. Only moments earlier those same brown eyes were pathetic and near tears. Kyle was responsible for the mess they were in and had begged for Adam's forgiveness.

When younger, the two brothers had constantly been mistaken for twins, but those days had long since disappeared. Adam had matured into a raven haired, handsome man. He was refined, graceful, and always in control. Kyle, on the other hand, was long and wiry and his face bore two sides: one of a small disillusioned child and the other of a man obsessed with his own destruction and the destruction of all around him. As Adam looked into the dark face he felt a sickening sour feeling in his stomach and looked away.

"Roll up your window for Christ's sake," he said quietly, as he reached his hand to his sweating brow. He stared out at the black bayou as it whipped past.

Kyle obediently closed the window while easily maintaining control of the speeding car. "Those old babies can fly, can't they?" he asked, looking anxiously over at Adam. He noticed the tiny beads of sweat forming on his brother's forehead.

Adam felt Kyle's scrutinizing gaze.

"What the hell are you looking at?" he demanded.

Kyle quickly put his eyes back on the road. Just then a rock spit up from the car in front of them and popped against the windshield. A tiny crack appeared at the base of the window and with each jolt ran slowly upward.

Slowly the dim tail-lights of the old car in front of them began to fade, then disappeared.

"We're losing 'em," Adam warned.

"I can't go any faster," Kyle said, keeping the gas pedal mashed to the floor.

Adam leaned even further forward straining to see through

2

the dark cloud. He clutched down on the leather dash as if the repositioning of his body would pull the car forward. "I can't see a damn thing," he grumbled, rubbing his eyes.

The outside roared past as the two men stared ahead in tense anticipation. Suddenly, the rear end of the old car was before them, completely still in the middle of the road.

"Watch out!" screamed Adam.

Kyle cranked the wheel to the side, narrowly missing the huge obstacle. He bore down on the brakes, but to little avail. The momentum of the Lincoln carried it forward. The tail end whipped around and they were soon spinning in a cloud of gravel and dust. Finally, as if stopping by choice, the Lincoln came to rest about a hundred feet in front of the old car, facing perfectly forward on the road. Kyle looked back in amazement.

"Am I good or am I perfect?" he asked in admiration of his maneuvering.

Adam, more concerned with the task at hand than Kyle's luck at driving, looked back through the settling dust at the old car sitting eerily abandoned in the middle of the road, the passenger door left open.

"Why the hell did they stop here?" Adam asked, looking about the surrounding swamp land. "There's nothing around for miles."

A smile made its way across Kyle's calculating face. He loved a good game of cat and mouse and the mouse seemed to be cooperating.

"Pure stupidity," he relished.

"Back up," Adam ordered, annoyed by Kyle's enthusiasm. It reminded Adam of the way their father was always in a good mood after disciplining them. Although he knew the couple had to be eliminated, he felt it somehow sinful to take pleasure in the undertaking.

3

Kyle put the Lincoln in reverse and slowly backed to the stationary car. As the car came to rest, Adam removed a pistol from his finely tailored jacket. Kyle quickly followed suit, removing a gun from under his belt, tucked in the back of his pants.

Adam looked over at his younger brother. "I fire the first shot," he warned.

The two men slowly stepped from the Lincoln, guns drawn, ready to fire. Adam led the way as they began walking toward the old car with the utmost of caution. As he drew near, he could hear the squeal of the car buzzer, apparently set off by the open door. The unnerving sound of the gravel crunching under his feet made Adam's heart race. It seemed like forever before he could see that the car was empty.

"Jesus," he whispered, annoyed by the violent thumping in his chest. He hated those rare occasions when he wasn't in control.

"Pull out those damn keys," he snapped.

Kyle grabbed the keys, immediately putting an end to the shrieking buzz.

"Look here," Adam said, pointing to the ground surrounding the passenger's side of the car. In the soft ground were several footprints leading into the dark swamp. Kyle smiled at the sight.

"Unbelievably stupid," he said, shaking his head.

"Come on," Adam said, leading the way into the swamp.

The two men quickly made their way through the thick cypress trees shooting up out of the marshy ground. They both hated the swampland, and were not the least bit interested in sticking around. Having been raised in the city of New Orleans, they found the unfamiliar sounds and darting terrain threatening, especially in the dark of the night.

Kyle followed behind his brother, jumping at every other sound, wheeling around with his pistol in hand. He was terrified of snakes and knew there must be one hanging from every tree and under every rock, waiting to slither onto the back of his neck or wrap its winding body around his leg. His most recurring nightmare was that he was backed against a wall and someone was holding a snake inches from his neck. He would stare for what seemed like hours into the beady eyes of the creature as its scissory tongue would come within a fraction of an inch of his skin. At all cost, he had avoided going anywhere that dream could possibly be realized. Now he found himself in a garden of reptiles where every hanging cypress limb was ready to coil.

"Jesus! Algiers is nothing compared to this shit!" he scowled, adrenaline shooting electrical shocks through his body. "At least there you know what you're shooting at."

Adam ignored the comment, continuing into the woods. He never looked back to their days in the New Orleans ghetto. Being one of the few who ever escape, he left his parents and that life when he was eighteen and had no intention of ever returning, even in his mind. Even though he had not seen his parents in over twenty years, he knew that Kyle went back often, and hated when his brother touched upon the forbidden subject.

*   *   *   *   *

Monique Sinclair wondered if she would ever see her baby alive again. The thought was so terrifying that she felt too paralyzed to move. She huddled in the upstairs attic of the old cabin, her husband, Charlie, at her side. They were huddled against a wall, periodically peeking anxiously through a clouded window to the outside. They had stumbled upon the abandoned structure about a mile from the road where they left their tattered Ford. While their clothing reflected extreme poverty, it also told of the colorful culture found in the southern Cajun territories. Although Monique, who was in her early thirties, was older than her husband, the only sign of the six-year age difference were the tiny lines etched around her beautiful emerald eyes. "Amy'll be okay, won't she?" she asked, even though she knew that he couldn't possibly have the answer.

Charlie looked quietly at his wife. He was stricken with how childlike she appeared hunched in the corner with only the moonlight to form her features. For the first time ever, she needed him to take command of the situation, and he was terrified that he would fail. Whenever a crisis had arisen in the past, Monique was always the strong one, the one who took care of everything.

"She'll be f-f-fine," he stuttered, instantly disappointed with himself for not being able to speak clearly even when his wife needed him more than ever.

Monique saw the sadness in her husband's eyes as he looked away from her.

"I love you Charlie," she whispered, turning his face back to her and smiling gently.

"I love you too, Moon," he said.

He took her strong hands into his own, and held them as if they were the finest of crystal. He looked down at her ungroomed nails and once again felt a desolate sadness. He had wanted to give her so much.

Just then, they both caught sight of the two men outside, quickly approaching the cabin.

Monique's breath instantly stopped. "Oh Lord Jesus," she uttered.

Charlie took his wife's face into his hands. "You s-s-stay here," he said, then gently kissed her soft lips.

6

"Don't go down there," she said. "If we wait here, they might not find us."

"Trust me," he said looking into her eyes.

Having no plan of her own, she had to believe in his new found assertiveness. "Be careful," she pleaded, as he once again kissed her. He smiled tenderly at her then disappeared into the dark attic in search of the stairs that dropped down to the floor below.

* * * * *

With daylight less than an hour away, the moon dipped toward the horizon, sending long night shadows across the dilapidated cabin. It would have been almost impossible to miss the oddly placed structure, which was nestled in a clearing on high ground, rising out of the swamp like a forgotten mistake abandoned by its unfortunate owners.

Relieved to be on somewhat safer soil, Adam and Kyle stood alongside one another surveying the cabin from a short distance. "Like sitting ducks," Kyle savored, cocking his pistol.

"I've got the first shot," Adam reminded, raising his gun and motioning for his brother to follow.

The two men approached the house from the rear, their foot steps dodging rotten boards that lay all around the fragile structure, which had been picked apart, one piece at a time, by the torrential southern rains.

Adam turned the knob of the back door, not surprised to find it unlocked. The rust ground inside the handle before giving way to his grip. He knew by the difficult turn that the handle hadn't been used for years and if the couple were inside, they must have entered from the front entrance. He creaked open the door, which led immediately into the kitchen. The air inside was musty and thick. He kept his gun poised in front of him as he moved into the cabin, keeping a watchful eye for the young couple. Kyle crept behind, also leading with his gun.

* * * * *

Upon hearing the back door squeak open, Monique made her way along the dark attic toward the ladder.

"Charlie?" she whispered out.

"Moon, stay there," she heard her husband whisper from below. She crouched down where she stood and waited. Through the slats of the floor, she could see the main room of the cabin situated below her. As she heard the men making their way through the kitchen, the boards beneath her began to creak as if to break. She looked down at the fragile old boards she rested upon, and saw that they were bowing. Just as she started to shift her weight to a more dependable piece of flooring, she saw Adam and Kyle enter the room and stop directly beneath her. She froze in terror, staring down at the top of the two men's heads as they stood in silence looking about the cabin. They were so close to her that she held her breath for fear the faint sound would give her away. Praying they wouldn't look up, she watched in anticipation of the worst.

"Check behind that stove," she heard Adam mutter. Just as Kyle began moving toward the potbelly stove, she was horrified to feel the boards beneath her give further. The sound of the splintering wood rang out through the cabin like a death toll imposed by a ruthless judge.

"What the hell was that?" Kyle asked, unaware of the floor above his head.

Through the cracks, Monique saw Adam turn his piercing eyes up toward her. The handsome gaze locked with hers, but only for a second before the flakes of rotted wood misted down into his eyes. He instantly turned away and began rubbing them in pain, trying to clear his vision.

Monique started to run, but the very movement thrust her downward.

Kyle looked up to see the ceiling above his brother rip apart, and Monique's leg break through. "Holy shit!" he exclaimed, rushing forward and grabbing the foot. He began yanking violently at the limb as if tearing down an unwanted branch from a tree.

Monique screamed, holding tight to a pillar which supported the roof. Her grip soon weakened under the powerful weight of Kyle's tugging. The pillar, abandoning her in the fight, burned across her hands, as she felt herself crashing toward the floor, her back abraded by the shredding wood. Her momentum was instantly stopped by the solid and ungiving floor of the cabin. Stunned by the impact of the fall, she looked up in terror at the brothers standing over her.

As the two men stared at the dazed young woman, a board came smashing into Adam's face, seemingly out of nowhere. He fell back against the wall, his gun dropping to the floor.

"Grab the gun!" Charlie shouted, slamming the board into Kyle's head.

Monique spotted the gun on the floor, and began scrambling toward it, but Adam was quicker. He reached the gun first, looking up just in time to see Charlie poised with the board in hand, again ready to strike.

Monique was horrified to see Adam raising the gun, the anger in his face directed toward Charlie.

"Noooo!!" she howled, moving with all her might to knock her husband out of the line of fire. Just then, Adam's gun rang out and the bullet pierced into her chest, sending her body back against Charlie. As she fell back into her husband's arms, she looked up at Adam, first with confusion, then disbelief.

Momentarily stung by Monique's incredulous stare, Adam faltered a moment, his gun falling to his side. "I didn't . . . " but the words were not there.

Monique fell to her knees and then collapsed on the floor as Charlie retrieved the board once more. Kyle, still on the floor, looked up to see Charlie ready to strike Adam again.

"Shoot him!" Kyle screamed, searching for his own weapon.

Adam, once again in motion, fired a barrage of bullets into Charlie's frail chest.

Monique, who lay helplessly on her stomach, screamed out in agony as her husband hit the floor beside her, his face within inches of her own.

"Charlie?" she said softly, her eyes fixed upon him. A prickling sensation crept through her body, as she watched a stream of blood trickle from his neck toward his collar. A tremendous sadness came over her as she looked into his eyes which were completely still. He had left her behind to face the darkness on her own and she felt so alone. She wanted to touch him, to hold his hand so he could be with her, but her hand wouldn't move. Just when the tiny red river reached the cotton of his shirt, the dark tingling within her slipped her into a deep sleep.

* * * * *

A muted orange glow sliced through the lace curtains, long since eaten away by time and countless moths. Adam could not believe the sun was already coming up. He hated dealing with this part of his business in the daylight. The night seemed to make things less confusing, rendering himself more efficient. He looked over at Kyle who was busy pulling Charlie's wallet from his pocket.

"You're not going to find fifty-six thousand dollars stuffed in his wallet for God's sake," he snapped.

"Do you want to do this?" Kyle asked, matching his brother's impatience.

Adam smoothed his hair and turned back toward the window, anything to avoid looking at the lifeless bodies. He loosened his collar, the smell of blood smothering him. He reached down to open the window, but it was jammed, sealed shut by years of lack of use.

"You said you already checked them for the money," he argued, keeping his back to Kyle.

"They may have picked it up after we left them in the Quarter," Kyle said.

"They're not gonna be stupid enough to carry that much cash," Adam argued.

"Well just don't be blaming me," Kyle asserted.

Adam turned to him with a vengeance. "Who the hell else am I supposed to blame?" he demanded. "You're the one who let 'em walk away with the money in the first place. Now I'll never get it back."

"Well if you hadn't killed them, we could have asked where

they put the money," Kyle countered, knowing full well that if Adam hadn't pulled the trigger, he would have killed them himself.

Kyle was relieved to see Adam turn back to the window with no response. Discussion closed, he thought, feeling very satisfied with the way things turned out. As long as the couple were dead, Adam would never know they didn't have his fifty-six thousand dollars.

"Cheer up brother, you'll make your money back when Marshal delivers the little angel," he said with a smile.

A shot suddenly rang out in the distance, echoing through the bayou.

"What the hell was that?" Kyle asked, looking toward his brother.

"I don't know," Adam said, noticing for the first time that there were a couple of bedrolls lying in the corner, along with a backpack. Kyle followed his line of sight.

"Oh shit!" Kyle exclaimed.

"They must be hunters," Adam concluded. "We've got to get those bodies out of here."

"What the hell are we supposed to do with 'em?" Kyle asked, obviously not enthused with the notion of bloody hands.

"Let's look around outside," Adam ordered.

* * * * *

For once in his life, Adam was grateful for the sticky air of the swamp. As he exited the back door of the house, he breathed a momentary sigh of relief. Even the stagnant air of the outdoors was better than the sweet smell of blood that was looming inside.

"Hey, take a look at this," Kyle called out, holding open a flat cellar door only twenty feet from the house.

Adam looked down into the dank hole that barely qualified as a cellar. Large stones held back the impending marsh, water having formed at the bottom of the enclosure.

"A cellar in the swamp," Adam said in amazement.

"Built by one imaginative boozer," Kyle admired, referring to the old wine jugs hung by ropes from the jutting stones.

A rickety ladder led down through the pit to the murky water.

"Couldn't have dug a better grave myself," Kyle smiled.

"Well, let's get on with it," Adam said, turning back toward the small house. Aside from not wanting to be there when the hunters returned, he intended to make it home in time for breakfast. Just the mere thought of rewarmed eggs and gravy caused his stomach to send a new batch of acid to his throat.

Adam winced upon entering the room where the bodies lay motionless. "How are we going to get rid of that smell?" he asked.

Kyle looked at him strangely. "What smell?"

"The blood," Adam replied.

"Since when did you get so squeamish? I can't smell anything," Kyle said. "Besides, those hunters will probably be so covered in it themselves that they'll never know the difference," he concluded, looking down at Monique's lifeless body. "Boy, she's a beauty," he said licking his lips. "It's too bad I'm not into necrophilia." He reached down and picked her up. "You should've let me have some fun before you shot her."

The smirk on Kyle's face, combined with the sight of the limp young woman dangling in his arms, hit Adam forcefully in the gut. "Put her down," he said in disgust.

13

Kyle looked at him a moment, as if wondering if his brother were serious.

"I said, put her down," Adam warned.

"Jesus, I was only joking," Kyle said, still holding the dead woman. Adam suddenly made a move toward him so he quickly laid the woman back down.

"Don't you have any respect?" Adam demanded. "We're not rapists for God's sake."

"I said I was only joking," Kyle repeated. "Where's your sense of humor?"

Adam said nothing as he reached down to pick up Monique.

"Oh yeah, I forgot. You never had one," Kyle said. "What's the deal with you and that chick, anyway?"

Adam turned his dark eyes up to his brother. "What are you talking about?" he asked, his heart suddenly beating out of control.

"I'm talking about the way you stood there like a zombie after you shot her. If I hadn't of yelled at you, Mr. Stutter Man would have played baseball with your brains," Kyle said.

Adam stood back up and looked at Kyle straight in the eyes. Did he know? No, he couldn't possibly have known that he slept with her the day she came in for the loan. "What's your point?" he asked, pushing to see whether Kyle really knew anything.

"Well, if I didn't know any better, I'd think maybe you had something going with her," Kyle ventured, not sure how far to push the limit, knowing well that his brother was a devout Catholic and abhorred adultery.

"And what are you basing this on, Einstein?" Adam asked.

Kyle hated it when Adam made reference to his intelligence, or perceived lack thereof. "Oh, I don't know . . . a feeling,"

Kyle said, suddenly feeling less confident.

"Well, you obviously don't know any better so I won't bust you in the mouth for accusing me of cheating on my family," Adam said. "But just so you have peace of mind, little brother, I shot her, didn't I?" he pointed out, momentarily getting used to the idea that he had killed her. Things always had a way of working out for the best, he told himself, trying to find strength in the fact that the young woman was dead. "Need I say more?" he asked, comforted only by the finality of the situation. "Now can we please get this over with?"

Adam reached down for the last time to pick up Monique. After a moment, Kyle reluctantly hoisted Charlie over his shoulder and followed his brother outside.

As Adam carried Monique toward the cellar, a strange feeling came over him again. A feeling of being out of control. He sped up his pace to reach the cellar quicker.

He looked down into the dark, dank hole and wondered what to do next. Just then, Kyle dropped Charlie's body down into the cellar without a moment's hesitation. There was only a slight splash when the cadaver hit the bottom, the water only a few inches deep. Kyle looked over at Adam.

"Well?" he asked.

Adam, not wishing to raise any more suspicion, dropped Monique as nonchalantly as possible. In spite of his effort to be casual, he felt a pang at the sight of her hitting the bottom of the pit. She landed on top of her husband, face up, the black water working its way through her long golden hair like dark slithering worms crawling toward her porcelain skin.

The heavy lid slammed shut, sealing the tomb in darkness, with the two motionless bodies left behind to be forgotten like old bottles of wine.

Chapter 2

Adam and Kyle were both exhausted from the long night and did not see Briggs inspecting the two abandoned cars until they were completely upon him. They were stepping out of the woods before either party noticed the other.

"Oh shit!" Briggs exclaimed, startled to see the two men emerge from the swamp. He instantly recognized the brothers and regretted leaving his gun on the front seat of his car.

"You gave me a start," he said, realizing he had stumbled upon a bad situation. When he saw the gun tucked in Adam's pants he thought about making a run for his car, but decided against it. Knowing that Kyle was the only one of the brothers who could possibly recognize him, he looked into his face searching for any signs of recognition.

"How you boys doing this morning?" he asked as casually as he could manage. Much to Briggs's relief, a friendly smile came across Kyle's face. He figured he must not recognize him.

"All right," Kyle said. "My car stalled and my brother here was just about to give me a lift."

Although Briggs knew that the beat up heap was not Kyle's car, and that something was obviously going down, his only goal was to get the hell out of there. He was not the heroic type, and at that moment felt ridiculously incompetent for leaving his gun in the car. Slowly, he edged backward.

"Well, I'll just head on my way, then," he said, reluctant to turn his back on the two men.

He hesitated a moment as if expecting to be stopped, then smiled and started to turn. Suddenly, Kyle pulled his gun from the back of his belt and fired a bullet into the man's head. Briggs's head popped backward, and after a stunned pause, he fell to the ground.

Adam could not believe what he had witnessed.

"Jesus Christ, Kyle!" he shouted. "What the hell did you do that for?"

"Don't you recognize an unmarked cop car when you see one?" Kyle asked, looking back at the boxy brown car. "He was the one following me around the other day, incognito. Hell, they're so obvious to me that they ought to put a sign on 'em saying 'Undercover Cop'."

Adam sighed heavily, worried that things were getting too complicated. He had never been involved with killing a cop before. Until then, there had never been any reason to.

"Now we have two cars to get rid of," he grumbled.

Kyle took a small coke vial from his jacket and opened it up.

"I've got just the remedy," he smiled, snorting some white powder from the container.

Adam looked at him in disgust.

"I told you not to do that crap in front of me."

Kyle held the vial to Adam's face. "Yeah, well this crap is going to save your ass."

"What the hell are you talking about?" Adam demanded, knocking Kyle's hand away.

"Well, first we got to get us another body and I think I know just where to find one. Follow me," Kyle said, making his way back down into the swamp.

Kyle led the way to the cellar where they had left the bodies.

Before approaching, they had carefully inspected the house for any signs of the hunters. Apparently the game must have been plentiful, because they still had not returned.

Kyle tugged at the heavy cellar door which resisted as if it hadn't been opened in thirty years.

"What the hell?" he grumbled.

Adam helped him pull it open, spilling light into the pitch black pit. The bodies lay in the water below, just as they had been left.

A shudder ran down Kyle's spine at the thought of descending into the hole to get Charlie's body. He knew snakes liked cool dark places and the cellar certainly qualified as that.

"I got a favor to ask," he said to his brother.

"No way. I'm not going down there. This is your hair-brained idea, not mine," Adam protested.

"Come on Adam, you know I can't go down there," Kyle pleaded.

"Oh, but you want me to?"

"Snakes don't bother you."

"There aren't any down there, look for yourself," Adam said pointing to the cellar. He looked back up to Kyle's pathetic face, and anger shot through his body. "It's that damned coke that makes you so paranoid," he said, acquiescing to the idea of retrieving the body from below, rather than arguing with his brother all day. "You're paying for this suit," he informed him as he began descending the rickety ladder.

Upon reaching the bottom, he stepped into the ebony colored water that immediately swished around his ankles. The encircling echo of dripping water which bounced off the cool dark walls made Adam feel off balance. He looked up at Kyle, who was leaning over the opening, silently watching from overhead.

"Get out of the light," Adam called, reaching down to lift the

18

dead man. With some effort, he managed to hoist him over his shoulder and get him up the narrow ladder. When Adam was close to the top, Kyle ventured to lean into the pit to pull the body up onto the ground. Adam, relieved of the weight, crawled out of the cellar, mud covering his suit. As he bent to wipe some of the sludge from his pants, he noticed a neck chain, containing a couple of trinkets, lying on the ground next to the cellar.

"What's this?" he asked, picking it up for closer inspection. At the end of the long chain there was a Saint Christopher's medal and an antique locket with a talisman etched into its face. Adam opened it up and inside there was what appeared to be an animal claw.

When Kyle saw the trinket in Adam's hand, he jumped back, almost falling over Charlie's body. "Holy shit! Drop it!" he exclaimed.

Adam looked at him strangely. "What's the matter with you? It's just a Saint Christopher's medal and a locket."

"Well the locket's not just a locket," he warned.

"What do you mean?"

"That claw inside is voodoo," Kyle said still keeping his distance. "It must have fallen off his neck," he said, looking down at Charlie's body. "It's got hexes and shit on it to protect the guy who wears it."

Adam chuckled and shook his head at the irony of his brother's statement. "Yeah, well a lot of good it did him," he laughed, looking down at the seemingly harmless figure engraved on the outside of the locket. He tossed the necklace into the pit, before dropping the wooden door shut. He looked up at Kyle who stood uneasily over Charlie's body.

"I'm not carrying him all the way to the car, if that's what you're thinking," he informed him, taking off in the direction of the road.

19

Kyle reluctantly heaved the body over his shoulder and followed Adam into the swamp. Although he was uneasy about the necklace, he had seen no other choice than to comply with his brother's wishes.

He carried the body through the sweltering woods, the rising sun causing the humidity to soar. When he lifted his hand to wipe the stinging sweat from his eyes, he nearly lost control of the weight braced across his shoulder. Quickly, he grabbed for Charlie's arm, and repositioned the increasingly heavy body. With his right hand clamped down onto the bare skin of the dead arm, he felt something move underneath. Terror shot through his veins, as he looked to the right to see a long snake coiled around the neck of the body, its tail stretched up along the dead man's arm, secured under his own grasp. He was paralyzed by the sight of the legless beast wriggling beneath his fingertips, its head twisting and turning only inches from his side. With his eyes riveted on the roaming head, Kyle was frozen in speechless horror for what seemed to be an eternity. Finally, adrenaline released his stricken muscles, and he thrust the dead body with the attached snake as far as he could, screaming in momentary madness.

"AAHH! . . . Goddamn! . . . Get it away! . . . Get it away!" he shrieked.

Adam looked around in time to see the snake unravel from the dead body which lay sprawled over a cypress stump. The tail slithered away, disappearing into the green floor of the swamp. Kyle, as pale as the cadaver, continued to panic, looking about his head and feet for any other possible attackers.

"Oh Jesus, get me out of here!" he cried.

"Kyle! Calm down!" Adam called out, trying to get control of his brother.

"Get me out of here!" Kyle screamed.

"Hey!" Adam shouted, grasping his brother about the shoulders and slapping him in the face.

The sting of Adam's hand brought Kyle back to reality and he managed to stop his hysterical ranting. He stood, soaked in perspiration, his body shaking uncontrollably. "It's the locket," he gasped.

"Get a hold of yourself," Adam said, reaching down to pick up the body. "You'd think this was the first time you'd ever killed anybody, for Christ's sake."

* * * * *

Upon reaching the cars, Adam dropped the body on the ground. "Now what?" he asked.

Kyle, who was still shaking considerably, stared down at the corpse as if hesitant to touch it. He looked up at Adam who was watching him impatiently. Finally, Kyle bent to the body and pulled it over next to the dead detective. He then removed his own gun from the back of his pants and handed it to Adam. "Wipe it off and put it in his hand," he said quietly, motioning to Charlie's body.

Adam wiped it with a hanky and then, careful not to leave any prints of his own, placed the gun in Charlie's lifeless hand. "Whatever you're doing, it better work," he warned.

"It will," Kyle said, slowly regaining some of his confidence. "Now, I'm going to hold up the cop while you take the gun in Sinclair's hand and shoot a bullet into him."

Adam looked at him with skepticism then placed his hand around Charlie's hand holding the gun.

Kyle pulled the detective up and held him awkwardly out to

21

the side of himself. "Okay, fire," he instructed.

Adam put his finger over Charlie's trigger finger and carefully aimed the gun at the detective's chest.

"Hurry up," Kyle huffed. "This guy's a tank."

Adam fired the gun, sending a bullet into the dead man's chest.

Kyle immediately let the body of the detective fall to the ground, then began searching him for a gun. To his amazement, there wasn't one. "What kind of idiot cop doesn't carry a gun?" he asked.

"Look in his car," Adam said.

Kyle spotted the gun on the front seat of the detective's car. He broke out into a laugh, his spirits rising again. "What a dumb son of a bitch," he said, reaching through the window. Upon closer inspection of the weapon, he smiled up at Adam. "Hey, boss, this may be our lucky day after all," he said.

"What's so damn lucky about it?" Adam asked, irritated by his brother's sudden mood shift. Ever since Kyle had started doing drugs Adam felt like he was dealing with a loose cannon. Suddenly, Kyle reached for Adam's gun, who immediately pulled back, guarding himself in reflex. "What are you doing?" he asked.

"Jesus. What do you think?" Kyle asked. "I'm gonna shoot you or something? Don't be so damn jumpy," he said. "Hold out your gun."

Adam pulled out his gun and held it out in the palm of his hand. Kyle put the detective's gun up next to it; they looked identical.

"You've both got .38's," Kyle said. "Smith and Wesson," he smiled, then took the detective's pistol and placed it in Briggs's hand.

"So what?" Adam argued as Kyle took the detective's hand

containing the gun and fired a bullet into the air. "If they check the bullets, they'll know they came from different guns."

"Pull him up," Kyle said, pointing to Charlie's body, not stopping to explain his plan.

Adam looked at Kyle a moment, his lips tense with forced patience. He knew he didn't have an answer to the problem at hand and resented the way Kyle always forced him to cooperate with his ridiculous schemes, instead of just explaining it first. He's always got to prove something, Adam thought, as he unwillingly stood the body of Charlie up by lifting him under the arms.

The moment Adam had hoisted the body into a standing position, Kyle let out a barrage of bullets that hit the dead body across the stomach and chest. Adam, taken off guard by the impact of the shots, lost his grip of the body and stumbled toward the ground. The bloody carcass followed him down, landing on top of him and pinning him against the dirt. "Stop, you stupid shit!" he screamed toward Kyle, who immediately ceased firing.

"With all those bullets to check," Kyle said, "if they even check 'em, I'd say the odds are now in our favor," he smiled, feeling he had successfully made his point.

Adam shoved Charlie's body off of him and rose to his feet. He angrily stepped toward Kyle and grabbed him by the jacket. "I ought to pelt you in the mouth," he said, his face only inches from Kyle's.

"I'm just doing my job," Kyle defended.

"Yeah, well, drop your smart-ass attitude or look for another," Adam warned. He looked at Kyle a moment and then shoved him roughly away. He glanced down at his bloodied suit. "You're lucky I keep a spare set of clothes in the car," he said. His gut ached again. He shook his head and concluded that if his brother didn't end up getting him killed, the acid in his stomach would do the job.

23

Kyle stood back and watched his brother fume. He felt stupid again. Even when his plans worked, Adam always made him feel like an imbecile. He pulled a packet of cocaine out of his pocket and put it on the body of Charlie. "Your basic drug confrontation," he said in almost a whisper. "They'll never question it."

Adam pulled open the trunk of his car. "Yeah, well they're going to question those tracks," he said looking down at the footprints leading into the swamp.

"I'll take care of it," his brother said.

Chapter 3

The radiant morning sun shone down on the gorgeous sprawling Claiborne mansion. The pillared beauty, built in the mid-nineteenth century, had survived the Civil War and many wars since, and bore a shield of honor awarded by the New Orleans City Council proclaiming it a historical landmark. As a teenager, Adam had often wandered up from the slums into the Garden District and stared for hours at the mansion, dreaming of the day he would own it. That day had come five years ago when he was thirty-three. Life would be happy there. Life would be perfect. Protected by its eight-foot iron gate and rolling lawns, it was to be his fort against the outside world.

Adam's Lincoln, still covered in dust from the night's prowling, pulled up to the security gate that immediately opened upon his arrival. He turned up the long drive, lined on both sides with huge oak trees that touched limbs at the top, forming a tunnel leading to the front circle drive. The catacomb of leaves had a soothing effect on Adam's weary mind. It had been too long a night with too many possible mistakes.

As he made his way across the wooden flooring of the generous porch, the front door gently creaked open and a black, elderly servant appeared as if on cue.

"Good morning, Mr. Claiborne," he greeted, immediately

recognizing that his boss had changed clothing since he left the house the night before.

"Good morning, Soley," Adam said, feeling his servant's gentle but scrutinizing gaze. "The dirty ones are in the trunk."

In spite of changing his suit in the car, Adam was unsuccessful in his attempt to erase all traces of the killings. As he passed through the doorway, Soley noticed dried blood on the back of his boss' neck. A sinking feeling filled the old man's heart. He truly respected Adam and tried not to believe the rumors he heard about town that his boss was a loan shark, with less than honorable dealings. He would defend Adam at all times, arguing that he was an oil man and had been ever since he began working for him ten years earlier. "An oil man," his friends would laugh. "Maybe he used to be, but the oil business ain't happenin' in these parts no more."

* * * * *

After having bathed and shaven in the comfort of a steamy bathroom, Adam stood before a full-length mirror fixing his tie. The bedroom behind him was furnished with the utmost of style, but was uninviting and cold. The high ceiling and towering windows made the room seem enormous, and empty. He pulled the tip of his tie to his belt, making sure it was the proper length, then checked his face for any possible razor nicks overlooked in the shower.

Even though Adam had a very appealing face, with a strong jaw line and eyes the color of mint, he could never see past the scar on his cheek bone. The scar was only an inch long, and to some would even add to his unconventional attractiveness, but to himself it was a marring reminder of his father. When he looked into the mirror, he didn't see himself, he saw an enemy.

Soley entered carrying a charcoal grey jacket, and held it out for Adam to put himself into. He brought the jacket up over his boss's shoulders, straightening it to a perfect fit.

"It looks like they got it right this time," Adam said, inspecting the newly tailored suit.

Soley smiled. His boss's broad shoulders and small waist caused an ongoing battle with the tailor. "Yes, they did, sir," he agreed.

Adam smoothed back his hair before placing the comb in his jacket. The elegant texture of the lapel brought about a lucidity to his movements. The previous night's events were suddenly more manageable, as if the suit itself possessed the ability to bestow confidence and control. Adam often mused what the world would be like if more people were given the empowerment of a nicely tailored suit—something he himself discovered in his late teens and had demanded ever since. In spite of his strong build, even in the sweltering heat of the summer, he would never remove his jacket in a business meeting for fear of appearing weak.

"I'll tell Mince to serve breakfast now," Soley said before quietly leaving the room.

* * * * *

A breakfast feast including steaming grits, eggs, sausage and biscuits, and all sorts of fruits were placed on the large mahogany table. Emily Claiborne was poised at the end of the table behind a plate that had been meticulously filled, its contents carefully scrutinized against their caloric content. She nibbled at the food, refusing to take her ice blue eyes off of the entrance to the dining hall. Her long nails moved gracefully over the plate, as she sat perched like a spider waiting for its prey. Observing all the social graces she had acquired, she ate slowly and gracefully, the main course yet to come. She had a matter to discuss with her husband. It was a matter which involved her very being—her upstanding position in the community.

Even if her son, Philip, had noticed the fury boiling in his mother's blood, he still would have continued his breakfast as usual. In the seven years he had been around, he had already started to develop his father's acidic stomach. He hated to eat, especially breakfast, because he always seemed to end up with a stomachache. He sat at the side of the table, placed perfectly in the middle, trying to figure out how to get out of eating the heaping plate his mother had fixed for him.

The moment Adam entered the dining hall he knew his wife had something on her mind. He looked at her briefly, then took his seat at the opposite end of the football field posing as a table.

Upon his father's entrance, Philip sat up straighter and looked even more intently at his food. He popped one of the shiny eggs staring back at him hoping to make it appear smaller, as if he were making progress.

"Mrs. Cleary called and said the baby is dead," Emily said, breaking the silence.

Philip looked up from his plate to see his mother staring at his father. He wondered what baby she was telling his father about.

Adam, startled by his wife's proclamation, nearly dropped

28

the spoon he had taken from the bowl of grits. "What?" he asked.

"She said that about an hour after Marshal dropped it off, it started coughing and the next thing she knew it wasn't breathing anymore," she said.

Philip instantly recognized the tone of his mother's voice. She only used it when he had done something wrong that needed an explanation. Judging by the fact that she was staring at his father, he thought his father must have done something to a little baby.

Mince, a large black woman, entered through the kitchen door, carrying another bowl of gravy. The tension in the room was thick as she quickly glanced about the table to see what needed refilling.

"Needless to say she wants her money back," Emily continued.

Adam felt his son's eyes upon him. "We'll discuss this later," he said.

"There's nothing to discuss. If you're going to be in the selling business, you have to stand behind your product," she insisted.

Damn her, Adam thought, anger shooting through his veins.

"Eat your food, Philip," he commanded, as if that would eliminate the child from ear shot.

Philip's stomach dropped. He had hoped his father wouldn't notice him. He sliced a piece of the egg-white and it slithered down his throat. He felt his father staring at him and knew that wouldn't be good enough.

"You're too damn skinny," Adam said, affronted by the sight of the sallow little boy.

"Can we stick to the subject at hand?" Emily requested.

Adam looked at his wife. "First off, I'm not in the selling business," he said. "It was my understanding that you wanted the child to have a better home."

"Not at the expense of social embarrassment. This kind of thing could ruin my friendship with the Clearys," she said, looking impatiently up at Mince who seemed to be hovering around the table with the bowl of gravy. "Just set it down," she commanded and then turned back to her husband. "Does she get her money back or not?" she demanded.

"Yes!" Adam said sharply.

Emily smiled and lowered her tone. "That's all I asked, dear."

Adam looked across the long table at his wife, who had returned to picking at her fruit. He watched her a moment in repugnance, then looked to his son who was slowly chewing his oatmeal. Adam couldn't understand why the child was so thin. He provided every kind of food imaginable, but he still refused to eat. The very sight made Adam tense.

"I told you to eat your breakfast," Adam thundered, deciding he wasn't stern enough with the boy.

Philip squirmed under his father's stare, the eggs and oatmeal swishing in his stomach making him nauseous.

Suddenly, a shriek cut through the air. Emily jumped to her feet, her white dress covered in gravy. Mince, the guilty party of the mishap, had already fetched a towel and was preparing to clean up the mess.

"Oh Ma'am, I'm so sorry . . . I didn't—"

"That's enough," Emily said quietly, her lips terse with anger.

Mince stood aside as Emily made her way around the table and toward the doorway.

"You're fired," she said, turning back to Mince, satisfaction twitching on her lips.

Philip felt sorry for Mince who ran from the room crying. He wanted to go and tell her that maybe it would be like the last time his mother had fired her. That she would be able to come back again. But instead, he recognized this as one of those inescapable mornings when he would have to finish his plate first.

Chapter 4

Adam pulled the Lincoln up to the beautiful, but ominously Gothic, St. Mary's Cathedral. Its spiraling steeple stretched toward the turquoise blue sky, the sun reflecting off the huge brass bell suspended within its stone columns. The grey gargoyles carved out of the cathedral's sides seemed strangely out of place against the bright day. They hunched menacingly on their hind quarters with their clawed feet poised to strike, frozen in motion as if waiting for the night to release them from the rock. Tulips and daffodils swayed in the garden beneath, softening the effect of the demon-adorned edifice. The dainty flowers were so lovely that most of the visitors were so distracted by the beauty at their feet that they seldom noticed the monsters looming over their heads.

Emily was seated next to Adam inside the luxurious Lincoln. She appeared to be in much better spirits after changing her dress. Philip was in the back seat, sitting anxiously forward, waiting for the car to stop.

After Adam had parked, Philip promptly exited the car and opened the passenger door for his mother. He was nervous with excitement but tried to be as grown up as possible. This was his first time to go to confession and he wanted to do everything just right. Every Saturday for as long as he could remember he had been left at home while his parents went to church to confess their sins. He was finally being included in the fun and he had no intention of messing it up. He took his mother's hand and walked up the long cobblestone path through the plush green lawns.

From across the path, a passerby admired with envy the perfect family as they made their way down the sunny walk toward the church entrance. They were a handsome family, polished to perfection, happily attending to their spiritual duties.

Once inside the huge archaic doors, the Claiborne family knelt in a long pew close to the confessional.

Emily looked about in search of a familiar face, her eyes finally landing on a wealthy widow. Satisfied at the juicy find, she began her favorite part of confession: trying to figure out what her fellow neighbor had to confess.

Adam looked down at his fidgety son who was faced with the dilemma of coming up with his own sins to confess. Being new to the ritual, he wasn't sure what qualified as a sin and what didn't.

"Stop fidgeting," his father warned.

Adam checked his watch and was irritated to see that it was already one in the afternoon. He was anxious to get back to the house to see if anything was on the news about the killings. Normally he wouldn't even bother, but this time a cop was involved.

He stared at the confessional door waiting for it to open. Losing patience, he looked about the familiar church. It seemed darker than usual. He watched an elderly man walk up to a statue and light a candle of vigilance. Adam looked closer at the statue, having never really noticed it before. He had been in the church hundreds of times and had never paid much attention to it. He looked closely at the eyes of the statue that towered over the small man. An uneasy feeling came over him as he thought of the figure etched on the locket he had retrieved from the ground in the swamp. It seemed to have that same foreboding appearance to it. He thought of how terrified his brother had been of the talon inside. Strange, he thought, that Kyle would turn his back on the church and yet believe in something as silly as voodoo.

Finally, the confessional door creaked open and an old lady with a tear-stained face exited.

* * * * *

Adam entered the confessional booth and knelt down in front of the screen. He could hear the faint voice of the priest talking to someone on the other side. As he waited in silence, his heart began to thump against his ribs. Jesus Christ, he thought, realizing that he was getting nervous. For the first time ever, he was scared to confess his sins. Not all of his sins, but one in particular. He had been unfaithful to his wife.

The priest's divider opened with a slicing motion. It's time, Adam thought.

"Forgive me Father, for I have sinned. My last confession was a week ago," he said, the sound of his own soft whisper making his heart race even more. He hesitated, unsure how to begin.

"Go on," the Father coaxed in a whisper, barely audible.

Adam couldn't seem to find the words. She's just a woman, he thought angrily, don't let her have this effect on you.

"Father, for the first time, I've committed adultery. I don't believe in infidelity to one's family. I know that family is everything, but there was something about this woman . . . I just couldn't stop," he said, embarrassed and humiliated by the thought of such weakness. "She came to me for a loan and when I asked for collateral, she offered herself to me," he confided softly.

He thought of her smooth skin touching against his cheek, the intoxicating smell of her sweat as she moaned in passion. A sharp pain made its way through his stomach. From his very first encounter with her, she had haunted him. He had hoped that the sex would put an end to his enthrallment with her, but it had only served to heighten it. He didn't understand his attraction to such a woman. She was trash, he said to himself, resenting being put in this position of weakness.

"Forgive me, Father," he said in resolution. "It's over now." Then, as if by rote, he listed the rest of his offenses. "I've taken the Lord's name in vain, several times. Also, as you know, the nature of my business sometimes ends in unavoidable death. There were three this week."

"You mean you took the lives of three people?" the priest asked.

Adam looked up upon hearing the priest's unfamiliar voice. He peered through the cloth divider and for the first time, made out the hazy vision of the person on the other side.

"Who are you? Where's Father Paul?" he asked.

"Father Paul is no longer with us," the voice answered.

"What do you mean?" Adam demanded, becoming increasingly anxious.

"He suffered a heart attack two days ago. My name is Father Jacob. I'm serving this congregation until his replacement is assigned."

Adam stood to his feet, feeling betrayed and angry at himself for being so careless. He never would have confessed had he known it wasn't Father Paul on the receiving end of his admission.

"What I've told you is guarded by your sacraments," he warned, taking the handle to leave.

"Your sins are safe with me, my son," he heard the priest say.

Adam hesitated a moment.

"Please stay," the voice requested.

Upon hearing the sincerity in Father Jacob's voice, Adam knelt back down. He ran his hand across his hair which had fallen down upon his forehead. He was uneasy and still unsure whether he should be confiding in someone he didn't know.

"I'm not accustomed to confessing to strangers," he admitted.

"I understand," Father Jacob said. "Perhaps, some are more forgiving than others."

"If you're referring to the three 'lives', Father Paul is aware of my work," Adam defended, feeling no further explanation was necessary.

"Did he forgive these murders?" the voice asked.

Adam resented the priest's choice of words.

"It isn't murder if you try to give someone a chance and they throw it back in your face. I help these people. I give them a chance," he insisted, starting to lose patience. "I have to protect my family. Now, what is my penance, Father?"

"You tell me that you haven't sinned, yet you seek absolution?" the priest asked. "I'm sorry, but I cannot give a penance to an unrepentant sinner."

Adam stared through the screen straining to see the owner of the low voice. Who the hell does he think he is, Adam thought.

"It's your duty as my confessor to absolve me of my sins," he said, the anger forcing his voice from a whisper.

"You can no longer hide under the skirt of the Church," the Priest said.

"Who are you to judge me? I'm an upstanding member of this parish," Adam said, insulted by the clergyman's insolence. "You're here to do a job. Now what is my penance?" he demanded.

"You're not sorry for the lost lives," the Priest countered.

"Give me a penance," Adam said, his anger measured and contained. "It's your job to give me a penance."

"Until you know the sorrows of your victims, your sins cannot be forgiven," the Priest said.

Adam's head began to pound and his heart race. He wanted to tear away the cloth divider, but the faint sounds of others in the church stopped him. He was not one for a public scene. "I'll be damned if I'll be told what to do in my own church," he said through gritted teeth and reached for the handle to the door. He swung open the tiny door with more force than he had intended. As it banged against the side of the confessional, every eye in the church was upon him. The inquiring faces caused his anger to mount. He was being humiliated by someone he had never even seen, an outsider who knew nothing about him. He had to see the pompous offender who was above the laws of the church. He reached for the door to the Priest's booth but it opened first. Adam was taken off guard by the sight of the priest already standing, waiting for the confrontation. He was an imposing man with a resolute face. Adam's eyes met the priest's with a vengeance, who stared back with equal determination.

The church took on a silence that was deafening.

"Adam?" Emily called quietly from behind him.

He turned toward her and saw that Philip was already in the other confessional waiting for the priest. Adam yanked open the door, revealing the small child kneeling within the booth.

Horrified by the sight of his angry father, Philip instantly thought he had done the confession wrong. He wondered what the consequences would be, as Adam grabbed him by the arm and pulled him to his feet.

"We're leaving," Adam announced to the stunned boy. He dragged him toward his wife, whose face was a mixture of shock and embarrassment.

Father Jacob, perched in the coffin-like confessional, watched with keen eyes as the family exited the church. His powerful hand went up to his chest and parted the black robes. From the folds he pulled an ancient, jeweled cross and he bowed his head.

"Tonight," he whispered, before closing the door once more to his concealed quarters.

Chapter 5

Kyle nearly choked on the pork-rinds he was eating when the newscaster began the top story of the night. He quickly grabbed for his beer to wash down the salty flakes. He had been waiting in front of the television for over an hour to see if his plan had worked.

A Police Academy photo of Detective Briggs covered the screen, as an announcer rattled off the story. "The off duty detective was on his way home when he encountered the suspect, Charlie Sinclair," the voice said.

Suspect, that's good, Kyle thought with relief.

In place of the detective's photo, a tanned, overly blonde newsman appeared. His shiny teeth flashed in a half smile that some newscasters always seem to use even when delivering serious stories. "Authorities believe that the young man's car was stalled on the county road, and the detective stopped to help. Upon finding the suspect in possession of cocaine and an illegal firearm, he made an attempted arrest, and a fight ensued," he continued.

Kyle jumped out of his lazy boy recliner in a pseudo-cowboy holler. "I did it!" he exclaimed.

"Authorities have been unable to locate Monique Sinclair, the wife of the dead suspect, therefore raising questions as to her possible implication in the crime. They believe she may have fled the state with their young child," the story concluded.

Things turned out better than Kyle had expected. They had even explained the whereabouts of Monique and the baby. Leave it to the cops to come up with a concoction like that, he mused, dialing the telephone to relay the good news to Adam.

* * * * *

Adam was relieved to hear the account, but at the same time hated that it came from Kyle. He had wanted to watch the news himself, but instead was forced by Emily's persistence to drive out to the Cleary residence; he was to pick up the dead baby and return the Cleary's money to them. Mrs. Cleary had wrapped the two year old toddler in a blanket and when Adam took it out to the country to bury, the quilt accidentally unfolded, dropping the small body to the ground. The sight of the little child lying blue and lifeless made him feel a pain he hadn't felt for years. He quickly wrapped it again, doing everything he could to erase the image from his mind.

As Adam sat on the side of his bed that night, he wondered if the baby would still have been alive if he hadn't killed its mother. Maybe the child would have died anyway, he thought, telling himself that Monique was a bad parent. At least he had given the child a chance at a better home, he convinced himself. He got up from the bed and put on his robe. He had been particularly uneasy all day. Thoughts of the priest refusing him a penance haunted him. He had never been refused a penance in his life. He hadn't murdered them, anyway, he told himself. It was self defense.

"That son-of-a-bitch priest," he mumbled aloud, pacing

about the room. "I give a lot of money to that church," he said to Emily who lay lounging in the bed with a magazine in her lap. "I don't have to stand for this kind of treatment. What kind of a priest is he?" he asked, working himself up once again over the incident. "Refusing to absolve sins. As if my dealings even qualified as sins," he fumed.

Emily was already bored with the conversation. She had heard it all day and was tired of it.

"So go to the All Saints parish," she offered. "I'm sure Father Bill would be more than happy to accept your 'atonement' check," she said snidely.

Adam looked at his wife as she plopped the magazine down onto the night stand and flipped off the light.

Chapter 6

Adam lay tossing and turning, a nightmare sucking him in and refusing to let him awaken. Remnants of conversations flashed through his mind like a roller coaster switching from one hellish track to another: the priest, ever looming, condemning him to darkness . . . Monique screaming as a bullet ripped through her husband, then her baby . . . the dead child falling into the cellar, a snake slithering down the wall toward it . . .

Adam bolted up out of the bed, his silk pajamas clinging to his body drenched in a cold sweat. He glanced about the room, breathing heavily. Moonlight streamed through the long elegant curtains painting the bedroom in a blue glow. He looked over at his wife, who lay sound asleep, undisturbed by his sudden movement. The clicking from the small clock on the night stand made Adam suddenly aware of the time. He was disappointed to see that it was only 11:55. It was going to be a long night, he thought.

His legs felt weak and shaky as he made his way toward the master bathroom that adjoined the bedroom. The cool marble floor of the bathroom sent shivers up his legs that felt like thousands of little needle pricks. He winced at the harshness of the light bouncing off the walls and mirror, as he opened the medicine cabinet in search of something to ease the night.

He opened the bottle of Valium and began to shake a couple

into his hand, but lost control of it and the entire bottle, contents and all, dropped to the hard floor with a crash. The pills flew everywhere, ricocheting off the porcelain fixtures. He looked down to his shaking hands, wondering what in the world was the matter with him. Unsure of the stability of his legs, he bent down and picked a couple of the pills off the floor, then filled a glass with water to wash them down. Even the tap water was shockingly cool to his body which again went into shivers. He thought to himself that he must have a fever and was probably coming down with the flu or something.

He looked at himself in the mirror and felt as if he were looking at a stranger. Beads of sweat covered his face and his eyes were sunken and dark, like those of a very ill person. Upon seeing his haunting image staring out at him, he turned on the water and splashed his face. He grabbed a towel and then returned to his bedroom.

His body ached as he lay back onto the bed, his skin feeling raw and exposed. He lay with his eyes open, staring straight overhead. The room felt enormous and dark, looming over him like a giant enemy. The bed began to tilt to the side, the long flowing curtains drawing nearer to him. His body tingled and his stomach churned while the Valium slipped him into a deep, all encompassing sleep.

He felt himself walking through the familiar dark swamp, a warmly lit lantern swinging back and forth in his hand, leading the way to the old cellar. He could not hear the wild sounds of the moor, only the sound of his own breathing touched his ears. His hand reached down and opened the door to the pit. The battered old hinges protested with a screeching wail that pierced through the silence. A booming thud replaced the high-pitched scream as the heavy door hit the ground. He leaned into the opening, the light of the lantern spilling into the black hole,

43

illuminating the body of Monique which lay lifeless at the bottom. She looked peaceful, her beautiful face enhanced by death, her long golden hair dancing in the water. To his amazement, her eyes slowly opened and she smiled a gentle invitation to him.

"Father Jacob said you'd be back," he heard her soft voice say seductively.

Her body began to move, lifting her into a standing position, then up the ladder to the opening. All the while she never took her eyes off of him. Entranced by her, he watched her muscular arms pull her up toward him with seemingly no effort.

She stepped out onto the ground next to him and stood before him, her damp dress clinging to her shapely body. He watched the water trickle down her neck and a rush shot through his body as her cold hand touched his, removing the lantern from his grip. She turned to walk away, looking back only to beckon him to follow.

Mesmerized by her invitation, he followed her to an old, willowy tree, where she hung the lantern on a limb, enveloping them in a warm light. She turned to him once more and he saw her bloodied dress.

He felt her icy fingers touch his chin and lift his face to meet her eyes. "You can make it go away if you want," she whispered. Then as if to show him, she slowly began pulling the dress up and over her body. As the fabric passed over her bare skin, no blood or bullet wounds were revealed, only her sensuously flushed body, no longer pale blue.

"See," she said, taking his hands and touching them to her bare stomach where the bullet holes had been. Her touch was no longer of ice, but warm and inviting. She brought his hands to her breasts, up to her neck and then to her lips. She gently kissed his hands, running her tongue softly between his fingers. She moved

44

closer to him pressing her body against him, her lips to his neck, then up to his ear.

"Give me back my life," she beckoned, her words echoing through his mind. Completely enraptured, he felt himself kissing her and then his hands moving wildly over her body.

"I love you," he heard himself say. "I've loved you from the first moment I saw you." He wanted her more than he had ever wanted anything in his life. He felt tears streaming down his face as he made love to her, shielded from the wild by the enrapturing light that surrounded them.

He heard her voice calling out, but wasn't sure what she was saying. Her body moved above him, her head thrown back.

"Charlie," she cried in ecstasy. "Charlie!"

"No," he said, opening his eyes and looking up at her, her body suddenly exposed in the daylight, drenched with sweat. A bed creaked below him, the sheets wrapped around his leg.

He was no longer in the swamp but in a small room. It all suddenly seemed so real . . . as if it were really happening. The sound, the light, the touch, the smell. The senses were so sharp, so vivid. Then his mind exploded as a shot of adrenaline rushed through him. It was really happening! He wasn't dreaming. He could see the room around him.

He looked up at Monique in horror, frantic with his seeming loss of reality. This can't be, he told himself, trying desperately to wake from the dream.

Monique stopped moving, staring down at him in confusion. The room behind her was dark, but warmly lit from the morning sun shining through the frayed curtains.

"Charlie, what is it?" she asked.

He shoved her aside and got up from the bed. The wooden floor was really there below his feet, he could feel it. He could see the old chest of drawers and the faded wallpaper on the walls. He could hear the sounds of a city through the open window. And Monique, she was really there, wasn't she? Maybe he hadn't killed her.

"Sweetheart, you're scaring me," she said, gathering the threadbare sheet to her body.

"Where am I?" he asked.

Monique stared back at him as if completely dumbfounded by his actions. "You're home," she said. "Charlie?"

"Why are you calling me that?" he demanded. "Quit calling me that!"

"Your stutter's gone," she said with astonishment.

"He's dead. You were both dead," he said. He suddenly felt naked and exposed before her. "Give me my clothes," he demanded.

She just stared up at him with the same bewildered look.

"Give me my damn clothes!" he exclaimed.

As if unable to grasp his bizarre behavior, she reached down to the floor and picked up a pair of jeans and held them out to him.

"Those aren't my clothes!" he screamed.

"I don't know what you want," she begged.

He grabbed the pants from her hands and quickly put them on, keeping his eyes upon her the whole time. He spotted a shirt and a worn pair of shoes next to a dresser. As he passed in front of the dresser mirror, he caught a momentary glimpse of Charlie moving simultaneously with him. He whirled around to look behind him, but only saw Monique still poised on the bed.

"Where is he?" he demanded.

"Who?" Monique asked, looking about the room.

"Your husband!" he exclaimed.

She stared up at him blankly.

46

"Charlie Sinclair!" he yelled.

She looked up at him as if he were crazy. She started to move toward him, but he moved backward.

He heard a noise behind him in the doorway and swung around violently to greet the intruder. His eyes fell upon Amy Sinclair, the tiny toddler he had buried the day before. Was it yesterday? He didn't know anymore. She stood frightened in the doorway looking up at him.

"Dada?" she asked softly.

It couldn't possibly be the same little girl, he thought, feeling as though he were losing his mind. He grabbed the shirt and shoes and ran from the bedroom down the hallway and into the living room. Nothing about the meagerly furnished apartment was familiar. He knew he had never been there before.

The front door to the apartment flew open and Adam raced out, down the dank hallway in search of an exit to the outside. Bare light bulbs hung from the water-stained ceiling, the floor beneath him creaking with every step. He could hear children crying, radios playing, and couples arguing. Private sounds of each apartment seeped through the thin, rotted walls of the building. A tall elderly black man stepped from his apartment door into the hallway, directly in the path of Adam. He had a look of grave concern on his withered face.

"Charlie?" he asked. "I heard shouting." But before he could question further, Adam brushed past in a hurry, desperate to see the light of the outside.

Pulling on the shirt, he flew down the stairwell, his only thought was to get into the open air. As he bound down the steps, two and three at a time, he could hear a saxophone wailing a sad, blues melody. Before he realized its origin, Adam tripped over the teenage boy who had been playing the instrument, and landed at the bottom of the stairs.

"Mr. Sinclair," the young boy said, leaping to his feet to help him up. "Are you all right?" he asked, looking into Adam's eyes.

Adam yanked away from the boy and burst through the fire exit door, sending off a belting alarm.

"You can't go out that way," the boy called to the fleeing man.

The glaring sun temporarily blinded Adam, as he made his way down the narrow alley way. From above him, he could hear Monique's voice calling out.

"Charlie!" she cried, leaning over a flower adorned balcony, but he didn't stop to answer. He quickly rounded the corner of the alley onto a main street. Oblivious to where he was going, he was nearly hit by a horse-drawn carriage. He looked up upon hearing the sound of neighing horses, who were reacting in anger at the sudden yank of the bit against their gums. The bare teeth of the horses flashed in his face, but were soon replaced by the smile of the black, colorfully dressed driver of the carriage. He laughed out loud at the sight of the disheveled Adam, before turning back to his passengers who consisted of tourists packed in like sardines.

"Folks, this is what happens after a night on Bourbon Street. The spirits steal your brain," he bellowed. Then he turned his wicked smile on Adam with a sentence of demise. "And some-times they don't give it back."

* * * * *

Adam could hear the carriage driver laughing as he turned to make his way down the street. He was in the French Quarter,

48

and had no idea how he had gotten there. The last place he remembered being was in his own bed at his mansion which was
miles from the Quarter. Judging by the light, it seemed like
morning to him, but how had he gotten to the Sinclairs' apartment?

He made his way frantically down the crowded street in
search of a taxicab. A sea of people with cameras moved past
him. The tangy aroma of spicy food and booze mixed with the
smell of body odor and clung to the stifling air. In spite of the
muggy heat, the tourists were in full force, each looking at him
as if he were an oddity. "He must be a local," he heard one
woman cackle to her husband. He suddenly became aware of
the old clothes he had put on. He looked down at his bare feet
and realized that he had forgotten to put on the shoes he was carrying in his hands. He stopped for a moment and tugged the
shoes onto his feet and much to his amazement, they were a perfect fit, the old leather nearly worn through exactly in the spots
where his skin touched the sides.

He spotted a taxicab and ran out into the street to wave it
down. Before the cab was completely stopped, he jumped into
the back seat and slammed the door as if barricading himself
from the overwhelming senses outside. As he sat down, he felt
the bulge of a wallet in his back pocket.

"Take me home, quickly," he ordered, pulling the annoying
billfold out and tossing it onto the seat beside him.

"I'm not a chauffeur, Jack, I'm a cabby," the driver razzed.

"4900 Chestnut," he said, trying to catch his breath.

"The Claiborne Mansion?"

"Yes. Now if you don't mind I'd like to get home," he retorted with little patience.

The cab driver looked curiously around at Adam's attire.
"Home?" he asked upon seeing the worn clothing and scruffy

appearance of his passenger. Then, as if finally understanding what Adam meant, he flipped down the meter and turned forward. "Oh . . . home," he said, with a measured amount of sympathy, before putting the cab in gear. "So what's your job at the Claiborne place?" he asked. "Does that asshole and his wife treat you as bad as they do the black folk in their kitchen?"

Unsure he had heard the driver correctly, Adam looked at the shining eyes of the black man in the rear view mirror. "What?" he asked faintly.

"My sister, Mince, works her fingers to the bone for that damn family with nothing to show for it," he said.

Adam felt indignant at the man's harsh words. "I treat my help with the utmost respect," he said, managing to locate his pride in spite of his slovenly clothes.

The cab driver looked back at him through the rear view mirror, confused by Adam's statement, then suddenly burst out into a raspy laugh.

"Oh, I get it," he said. "I treat my help with the utmost of respect," he imitated. "That's funny."

"Just shut up and drive," Adam ordered, stung by the cab driver's misinterpretation of the situation. He felt tired and just wanted to get home and take a shower. Then he could relax and try to sort out the strange turn of events.

He noticed a newspaper lying on the seat next to him. He recognized the paper as being an old one.

· "Pull over at the next newsstand. I want to get a paper," he ordered.

"What's wrong with the one you got in your hand?" the cabby asked, looking through the rear view mirror.

"It's three days old," he answered.

"No it's not," the cabby said. "I bought it myself just this morning." A smile of pride made its way across his pudgy face. "I provide them for my customers."

Adam recognized the newspaper as being last Thursday's, but checked the date just in case he was mistaken. "Like I said, it's old. Now pull over," he commanded.

"Whatever you say, mister," the cabby mumbled, pulling the taxi up to a curbside newsstand.

Adam started to exit the cab, but upon seeing that the same paper was in the machine, he shut his door once more.

What the hell was going on? It was Sunday, not Thursday. He couldn't have lost track of three days! He looked down once more to the paper in his hands. He flipped through the pages, scattering it about the back seat. It couldn't possibly be that day's paper because he had already read it!

Adam noticed the driver staring at him strangely in the mirror. "Have you got a problem" he asked.

"No, sir," the driver said, putting his eyes back on the road.

Chapter 7

Adam was relieved to see the mansion in sight, a landmark of stability. "Pull up to the gate," he ordered the driver, pointing to the entrance along the wrought iron security fence guarding the mansion.

The taxi came to a halt and the driver pulled down the meter. "That'll be $8.75," he said.

"I don't have any cash on me," Adam said, opening the car door. "Just take it out of what your boss owes me."

The driver turned in his seat as Adam got out of the taxi. "Hey buddy, I don't know nothing about what my boss owes you," he argued.

"Well I do. Just tell him Adam Claiborne had a free ride. I'm sure he won't mind," he said and then slammed the door.

"Adam Claiborne, huh?" the driver asked with a chuckle.

Adam looked back to see the driver looking as though he were waiting for a punch line.

"That's right," he snapped, his patience worn down from the trying morning.

Upon seeing that his passenger was serious, the smile faded from the cabby's face. "If you don't pay, I got to pay," he said, his good humor replaced with slight panic.

Adam looked down at the wallet lying on the seat where he had pitched it. He reached through the back window and-grabbed it, quickly opening it to search for any wayward cash. He pulled apart the bill compartment, finding two one dollar notes. He shoved them toward the driver.

"That'll have to do," he said pointedly, throwing the wallet to the ground beside the taxi. He quickly walked over to the security gate and hit the buzzer.

"Let me in, Eli," he said into the speaker.

The deep sound of Eli, Adam's security guard, came over the small box. The natural base of his voice vibrating the metal casing.

"Can I help you?" he asked.

"This is Adam," he said. "Open the damn gate." He stood back and waited for the gate to open. After a moment, he hit the buzzer again.

"Hey," he heard the driver call from behind him. "Either pay up or I call the cops."

The anger rose in Adam's chest upon hearing the driver's words. The owner of the cab company owed him a lot of money and he didn't appreciate the driver's disrespect. He walked slowly toward the cab, then leaned into the driver's window. "Are you threatening me?" he asked in a low voice. The driver scooted back in his seat to put distance between them.

"Look, mister, I don't want no trouble," he said, the situation resembling the time he was belted by an angry customer.

"Good," Adam said with finality, looking him squarely in the face. He abruptly stuck his hand inside the window, moving in the direction of the cab driver, who shrank back in his seat, shielding his eyes from any possible blows. Adam bore down on the horn of the cab, and held it down for several seconds, while looking toward the mansion. After a painfully loud moment, he let off the horn and once again rang the security buzzer. There was no answer. He pressed it again, then again and again, until finally, Eli's voice returned to the tiny speaker.

"If you want to see Mr. Claiborne you'll have to go through the proper channels," he said.

"Eli, you dumb bastard, what the hell are you talking about? This is Claiborne," Adam shouted, losing the battle to control his temper.

The monitor immediately let out a blip to announce that communications had come to a halt. Enraged, Adam began pounding the speaker. "Eli?!" he called, banging the speaker with all his might. "Open the gate!!" he screamed, continuing to pound the box as if the blows would reach the vanished voice.

Inside the cab, the driver picked up the handle to his radio. He spoke quietly into it, keeping his eyes on Adam who had his back turned toward the taxi.

"Dispatch, this is 128. I need the assistance of 10-3. I'm not sure if I got a 10-2, but I definitely got a 10-7 on my hands out at the Claiborne Mansion on Chestnut Road," he said.

"10-4, we'll handle it," squawked the response from his two-way radio, then he quickly returned the hand unit to its position on the dash.

Adam realized that he was getting nowhere and stood back a moment to catch his breath. He looked toward the mansion that seemed to be taunting him with his own security system, as if it had joined forces with the other bizarre events of the day. He looked back to the cab driver who instantly looked away, avoiding eye contact with him as if he were dangerous.

"Jesus Christ! I don't believe this," he hissed as he began scaling the large oak tree that stood next to the fence. Having had over two hundred years of growth, the live oak's branches spread out over the sky, reaching out like a giant creature with twisting, turning tentacles. It had been a long time since Adam had climbed a tree, but luckily his ascent was eased by the long arms of the oak stretching down to the ground as if to pick him up. Once over the fence, he saw that the limbs on the other side didn't afford the luxury of an easy descent.

"Son-of-a-bitch," he mumbled, looking down to the hard ground below. He felt ridiculous for having to crawl over his own fence, and would feel even worse if he ended up breaking bones in the process. "Just wait till I get a hold of that damn Eli," he muttered, then took the leap.

* * * * *

In spite of Eli's menacing and muscular appearance, he was not the sort of security guard who welcomed trouble. As a teenager, his body had betrayed him time and time again when some young bully would mistake him as a threat to their manhood and challenge him to a dual of testosterone. Even though he often lost, he still seemed to attract the seedier vein of society; they just couldn't accept that a man with the face of a huge bat and the body of a gorilla possessed a gentle soul. Fortunately, after several years of suffering at the hands of men smaller than himself, he adopted the killer instinct expected of him, and went on to become, if not an enthusiastic security guard, at least a reliable one. For several years he had worked at the Claiborne mansion, his small quarters inside the gate a safe haven with little or no trouble.

That morning, he sat inside the little cubicle, staring out at the gate, hoping that whoever the pissed off person was on the other side, would just go away. He heard the blasting horn and cringed at the thought of his boss also hearing the noise. When the caller buzzed him again, he tried to be forthright and to the point, hoping he would leave, but he didn't. Although he didn't see who the intruder was, when he saw him climbing over the gate it reminded him of Charlie Sinclair, who had arrived unannounced last week at the Claiborne home. Sinclair had come to the house regarding a loan his wife had taken out, and Mr. Claiborne had given strict instructions to never let him in again. "I don't want anyone coming through that gate unless I know who they are and what they want," Mr. Claiborne had ordered not more than a week ago.

Eli thought about calling up to Mr. Claiborne's bedroom, but hesitated in case Claiborne hadn't heard the horn and was still asleep. While battling with the decision of whether or not to disturb his boss, the telephone in his security booth rang. As his large hand reached for the receiver, his stomach dropped to the floor in dread of the voice on the other end.

"Yeah?" he said into the mouthpiece, his meek tone a strange contrast to his gnarled knuckles that clutched the phone.

"Eli, what the hell is going on down there?" the voice demanded into his ear.

"I think it might be that Charlie Sinclair guy. He's climbed over the gate. Do you want me to call the police?" he asked.

"No, don't involve the police. Just get him off the property," the voice ordered, then the line clicked.

Shit, Eli thought, grabbing his shotgun.

* * * * *

As Adam walked quickly toward the mansion, the anger welled up inside him causing his breathing to speed up even faster. He stepped up onto the wooden planked porch and

56

pounded on the front door. He didn't bother seeing if it was un-locked because he himself had given the order to Soley to al-ways keep it locked. After a few seconds the ornate brass cover-ing to the peep hole swung open and Soley looked out at him.

"I'm sorry sir, but Mr. and Mrs. Claiborne are not accepting visitors at this time," he said to Adam's astonishment. Before Adam could respond, Soley shut the peep hole.

"Soley?!" Adam screamed, tired of whatever joke they seemed to be playing. "Soley, let me in before I break your stinkin' neck," he threatened, pulling back his fist and pounding the door with all his might. After several blows, his hand began to ache, further feeding his furious heartbeat. He stood back to catch his breath and bent over like a racer after a quarter mile sprint. Drops of sweat spattered onto the floor beneath him, as he desperately tried to calm himself. "I'll just fire them," he told himself, somewhat soothed by the promise of retribution. After a moment, he straightened back up and at the sight of the locked door in front of him, the fury returned with a vengeance. He picked up a large planter containing ivy and heaved it through the front window that stretched along the side of the door. The tall window shattered to the floor, shards of glass falling like daggers. After looking at his handiwork, he began to step through the new entryway, but stopped upon hearing the sound of a shotgun cocking behind him. He whirled around in anger.

"What the hell is going . . . " but the disbelief in what his eyes were showing him caused him to stop in mid-sentence. Eli was pointing the barrel of the shotgun straight at him.

"This is private property, sir. Get your butt out of here or I'll blow your brains out," he warned.

"Have you gone mad?" Adam asked in amazement. It was clear to see that Eli had indeed been pounded in the head too many times and had finally snapped. "You're fired," Adam said, then turned back to the window to climb through, but was immediately pulled back by the security guard's powerful grip. He felt himself being dragged off the porch like a rag doll with no chance of escape. Eli hurled him through the air to the foot of the stairs, his body landing on the gravel walkway. He looked up to defend himself against the ape, but his eyes were caught by someone standing in his bedroom window upstairs looking out between the parted lace curtains. As the features of the figure came into focus, Adam fell back, stunned by the sight he immediately recognized. It was the ruthless face of himself, Adam Claiborne, standing in the window staring back down at him. He lay paralyzed, an icy chill consuming his very being. The figure stepped back from the curtains which quickly closed in callous finality.

Suddenly, Adam realized that he was being dragged from the house by Eli. He started to struggle, but his legs were limp beneath him, all his energy drained by the stunning sight of the figure in the window.

Someone is in my house, he thought.

"Is this some kind of a joke?" he demanded trying desperately to get to his feet, but Eli was unrelenting. "What's going on? Get your hands off me you dumb ox!"

He heard the piercing sound of a siren as Eli dragged him through the gate, which now stood open. He tried once more to gain his footing but before he could, he was lying face down in the dirt outside the estate. The gate slammed behind him as a police car pulled up almost running over his head. He tried to wipe the dust from his eyes in order to see more clearly the officer getting out of the car only a couple of feet away. As he moved his hand up to his eyes, his shoulder gave him a sharp pain. He must have landed on it, he thought.

"What seems to be the problem, gentlemen?" he heard a

woman's voice ask. It was the officer closest to him. Her badge read Officer Fritz.

Another officer exited the patrol car and stepped up to the taxicab, which was still parked in front of the gate. He reached down and picked the wallet off the ground where Adam had thrown it.

"No problem, he just has the wrong address," Eli said through the wrought iron gate, before turning around and heading back to the mansion.

"I've got a problem," the cab driver piped in. "He still owes me six seventy-five."

The male officer was looking through the wallet he had retrieved from the ground. "Is this yours?" he asked Adam, who stood shakily to his feet.

"No, but this is my house," he answered.

A smile came across the officer's face. "Yeah, right," he chuckled.

The cab driver, getting braver by the minute, stepped out of his car. "It's his wallet. I saw him throw it down," he informed the officer.

The officer pulled the driver's license from the wallet and compared it to Adam. "It's his all right," he said to Officer Fritz, handing her the license.

"It's not mine," Adam defended. It couldn't be.

Officer Fritz looked at the driver's license photo of the blonde-haired, blue-eyed Charlie Sinclair. She looked up to Adam standing in front of her and saw that it was indeed the same person. "Yep," she concluded and handed the license to Adam, who quickly looked down at the card.

"Are you blind?" he asked seeing that it was a picture of Charlie Sinclair. "This guy has blonde hair. Mine's almost black!"

The two officers looked at the blonde-haired man in front of them and smiled.

"He's a little daft if you ask me," the cab driver volunteered.

"You shut your mouth," Adam ordered, before turning back to the officers. "Look, my name is Adam Claiborne and I live here. If you'll let me go inside to get my wallet, I'll prove it to you," he said.

The male officer took a pair of handcuffs from his belt. "Are you going to pay the cab driver or not?" he asked.

"My money is inside," he answered.

The officer stepped toward him, but Adam stepped away.

"Mr. Sinclair, you don't want to resist arrest," the female officer warned.

"This is insane," Adam protested, complying with the officer who snapped the cuffs tightly around his wrists.

"You have the right to remain silent. Anything . . . "

"This is my house! My wife is inside. She'll tell you . . . " Adam pleaded as he was shoved inside the back seat of the police car and the door slammed in his face.

His shoulder ached as if he had broken it. He scooted around in his seat trying to relieve the pressure the cuffs were causing on his shoulder joints. His arms were stretched back so tightly that his chest felt the pressure like a fragile wishing bone in the hands of an enthusiastic child.

He watched out the window of the patrol car as the officers spoke to the cab driver. He couldn't believe he was being arrested for a six dollar cab fare right outside of his own home. And arrested as Charlie Sinclair of all people!

Had the whole world gone mad overnight? Oh Jesus, he thought. Eli and Soley. They had worked for him for years.

They had always been so trustworthy. What the hell happened? It was as if they really didn't recognize him. The image of himself standing in the window flashed through his mind. Son-of-a-bitch! There's someone in my house, he thought.

"Hey," he called out, but the officers didn't hear him. The window was up and he had no way of opening it.

"Hey!" he yelled louder and the male officer looked around. He made his way to the driver's side.

"Pipe down, mister," he said sliding behind the wheel.

"There's someone in my house," Adam said.

Officer Fritz got in the car on the passenger's side.

"Yeah, the owner," the officer said with sarcasm.

"I'm the owner," Adam said, feeling as if he wanted to belt the cop. "I don't know who he is but he looks just like me. My security guard must think he's me."

Officer Fritz looked back at him with a mild look of sympathy. "Maybe this one ought to go to county," she said to the officer as if Adam weren't present.

"No, let's take him in, anyway," the male officer responded.

"Just listen," Adam ordered. "I know this sounds weird, but I woke up in this other guy's bed and I didn't have my own clothes so I used his. When I got home my security . . ."

Wait a minute, he thought. Just keep your mouth shut until you talk to your lawyer. This must be part of some weird set-up to get me to confess to killing the Sinclairs. Monique must have survived somehow and gone to the police. But what about the baby standing in front of him in the bedroom that morning? He had felt its cold body. He had buried it the day before. Or did he? Oh Jesus, he thought, laying his head on

61

the back of the seat. He didn't know what to believe. This can't be happening, he told himself, staring up at the gray ceiling of the squad car as it moved down the road.

The two officers were in the front seat talking and occasionally laughing, but Adam no longer heard them or even noticed them. They were merely part of a twisted reality that moved about him and propelled him forward.

Chapter 8

The car came to a halt and the door next to Adam opened.

"Let's go inside, Mr. Sinclair," Officer Fritz said, holding the door open for him.

AAAhh! The pain shot through his shoulder and down his back like a stinging fire inside his muscles.

"Are you all right?" he heard the officer ask.

"It's my shoulder," he said.

The officer reached down and helped him from the car.

"We'll have someone look at it after we book you," she said.

"I've got my own doctors, thank you. Just get these cuffs off," he said in disgust.

* * * * *

"Don't book him yet. I want to have a little chat with him first," Sergeant Hadley ordered the young officer standing before him in the busy station. "I'll meet you in the questioning room," he said, before making his way toward the long, barren room.

A couple of weeks earlier it had been called to the Sergeant's attention that a resurgence of organized crime may be brewing in the streets of New Orleans. Over the previous few months there had been complaints from various shop owners and passersby who had witnessed the beating of their neighbor and called the police thinking they were doing the victim a favor. When the officers would arrive, the bleeding victims would deny the involvement of an attacker, concocting stories of domestic accidents to explain their injuries. One middle-aged tavern owner even suggested that he had fallen and hit his head twelve times to account for his multiple head lacerations. Since the victims were never willing to say what really happened, the officers were forced to accept their stories of gross clumsiness.

After the number of reported assaults increased to an annoying amount of wasted police time, the Sergeant decided to look into the matter a little deeper himself. He noted that although the beatings took place all over the city, the sightings often had one thing in common: according to some of the eye witnesses, the aggressive attacks were allegedly performed by Kyle Claiborne and his partner, Marshal Long. After looking up the suspects, he discovered that Kyle had been brought in before on possession of cocaine, but never served any time due to a top dollar lawyer who got him off on a search and seizure technicality. His partner, Marshal Long, on the other hand, had an extensive record, all charges relating to assault and battery. In Long's fifty-four years of existence, he had acquired a lengthy resume of brutality by working with various loan sharks. Some speculations were even made as to his involvement with the mafia, but nothing solid ever substantiated that claim.

When the Sergeant had looked up Kyle's record, he noticed that he was an employee of his brother, Adam Claiborne, who was well known for his wealth accumulated from the oil business around New Orleans. Kyle was supposedly a monkey man on a rig that his brother owned. The only problem with this account of his earnings was that most of the oil companies out of New Orleans had gone belly up, and Claiborne had only one rig left in operation after the oil bust of the mid-eighties. Although that rig was reported to still be operating, there hadn't been any records of crude sales to the local refineries in several years, fueling the speculation that Claiborne had actually capped the well, awaiting an improvement in oil prices. Even if the rig had been pumping, the Sergeant deduced that it would certainly not be an operation large enough to support Kyle's colorful lifestyle, or Claiborne's ever mounting fortune. The Sergeant knew their income had to be coming from another source. The collapse of the oil economy had been devastating to Louisiana, causing bankruptcies, layoffs, and general hard times. Not surprisingly, banks were hit the hardest, now holding worthless portfolios of oil and real estate loans from insolvent companies and individuals. Facing tough federal scrutiny, the banks were forced into a conservative lending mode, further tightening the already tough economic situation and laying the perfect foundation for a lucrative loan sharking business. Who else would recognize this opportunity better than a man affected by the bank regulations himself: a man like Adam Claiborne?

Although there were several indications that the Claiborne brothers were more than likely up to the illegal activity of loan sharking, the Sergeant still couldn't justify a lengthy investigation, unless someone was willing to come forward and testify.

That morning, when Sergeant Hadley heard that a man from the French Quarter had been arrested outside of Adam Claiborne's mansion, claiming to be Adam Claiborne, he decided to speak with him himself.

As Officer Fritz led Adam through the doorway into the

brightly lit room, the Sergeant instantly recognized the man before him as the sax player who worked in a bar he often frequented.

"Take a seat," Officer Fritz instructed Adam, pointing to a chair alongside a narrow table.

Adam looked uneasily about the room. "Don't I get a call?" he asked defensively, still standing.

"No need to worry Mister . . . " the Sergeant looked to the officer.

"Sinclair," she offered.

"Sinclair. I just want to ask you a few questions first," the Sergeant said.

Adam reluctantly took a seat while the Sergeant looked over the arresting report.

"Adam Claiborne, huh?" the Sergeant asked looking up at Adam with a chuckle. "Why the hell would you want to be that thieving bastard?"

"I've got a right to a lawyer," Adam said.

The Sergeant studied the man before him. "There may be no need for an attorney. We may not even book you," he said adopting a tone of comradery. "Hell, Mr. Sinclair, I've heard you play down at Jimmy Blues. You're pretty good."

Adam looked up at the Sergeant, tired of the relentless, tiresome day. "Look Mister, whatever the hell your name is. I don't know what kind of stunt you people are trying to pull, but my attorney is going to have a field day going after your officers for arresting me outside of my own home under the name of a dead man," he said.

The Sergeant and Officer Fritz looked at Adam in slight confusion.

"What do you mean a dead man? Are you trying to say that

Adam Claiborne is threatening your life?" the Sergeant asked hopefully.

Adam looked up at the Sergeant and spoke slowly and deliberately. "You know damn well that I'm not Sinclair and that my name is Adam Claiborne. And you also know that Sinclair's body was discovered yesterday, on a dirt road outside of town."

There was a moment of silence as the Sergeant stared back at Adam with a confounded look on his face. He then turned to his officer for answers but she only shrugged her shoulders.

"What? You think I don't watch the news?" Adam asked in amazement. "Look, if you want to charge me with something, do it. But I'm not saying anything else until I talk to my lawyer," he insisted.

"What the hell is he talking about?" the Sergeant asked Fritz.

The officer looked angrily at Adam, unwilling to take the blame for the prisoner's strange behavior. "We've got your identification, Mr. Sinclair. We know who you are."

Adam sat obstinately in his chair staring forward.

The Sergeant took a seat opposite Adam and sat quietly for a moment watching him. Adam looked at the Sergeant, apparently uncomfortable with such close scrutiny. The Sergeant noticed sweat forming on the young man's forehead. "Mr. Sinclair. You're obviously trying to confuse the issue here and I must say you're doing a good job. What I think you need to understand is that if by chance you went to Claiborne's house this morning to do business with him, there's nothing we can do to you for borrowing money from the asshole. All we want is information on him and his brother Kyle," he said. "They've hurt a lot of people."

Adam continued to stare ahead in silence.

After a moment, the Sergeant turned to Officer Fritz with a heavy sigh. "Lock him up," he said.

"What do I charge him with?" she asked.

"Not paying the taxi," the Sergeant replied, before turning to Adam squarely. "If you decide to tell us what you know, we can protect you from his thugs. Hell, I'll even pay the cabby myself," he offered.

* * * * *

Maybe I said too much, Adam worried, as they rolled his hand print over page after page of paper.

"Go wash your hands at that sink," the officer behind the glass ordered.

Adam made his way over to the sink, his mind reeling with anxiety. What if they really did think he was Sinclair? But they found his body, he argued to himself. Or did they? Maybe Kyle was full of shit. Maybe it really wasn't on the news that they had found the detective and Sinclair. It was possible that Kyle just said that to get himself off the hook for being so careless in covering things up. But that still wouldn't explain why the hell they thought he was Sinclair. Nothing added up to him. It seemed the more he thought, the less things made sense. He turned on the water and rubbed the soap between his hands while he looked about the station. A day by day calendar hanging on the wall showed that it was Thursday. Again, Thursday. Christ, he thought.

"When do I get my call?" he asked the officer in the last window.

The officer looked up from his paperwork, the fluorescent light tinting his spongy complexion green. "When we're good and ready," he responded, before shining the top of his bald head once again at Adam.

After a moment, the officer reached over and hit a buzzer which released a large door.

"Make it short," he ordered without looking up.

Adam walked through the door and immediately saw the phones inside the hallway. He picked up the receiver and started to dial and then realized he wasn't sure who to call. If it were some kind of twisted setup, maybe he shouldn't call his wife. Maybe she was in on it. Maybe not. Shit. Play the safe side and call Teddy Graves. Nothing beats a good lawyer.

When the familiar voice answered the phone, Adam's spirits were suddenly lifted. Graves had been a friend since childhood, helping in all legal matters as far back as he could remember. He had even helped Kyle get released from the narcotics charge.

"Teddy," he said, "Hi, this is Adam. Listen, you've got to help me out."

There was a pause on the other end. "Who is this?" the voice asked.

A sinking feeling came over Adam. "This is Adam, Teddy," he repeated, trying to sound casual.

"Adam who?" the voice asked suspiciously.

This can't be happening, Adam thought. "Claiborne," he said, his voice rising.

There was silence on the other end.

"Who is this?" the voice demanded.

"Teddy, don't you recognize my voice?" Adam begged.

The line clicked.

Panic began to invade Adam's mind. What was happening

to everyone? To him? If Teddy wouldn't help him, who would?

"Sinclair," a voice from behind called as if it had been there for some time waiting.

Adam looked up in a daze.

"Let's go," the officer said and began leading him down a hallway to lock up.

Chapter 9

The clanking of keys on metal brought Adam out of his deep
sleep. He looked about, disoriented by the enclosing cement
walls and the foul stench. Then the realization of where he was
slammed him in the face when a cold stream of saliva oozed
across his forehead, from the bunk overhead.

"Goddamn it!" he yelled as he looked up to see a drunk
hanging over the upper bunk. The drunkard's eyes opened with
a red glaze and looked down at him, as Adam scrambled to
miss the ever flowing stream of drool.

"You've been bailed, Sinclair," he heard someone say as he
got to his feet. He wiped the sticky slobber from his face and
looked over to see a guard on the other side of the bars opening
the door to the cell.

Adam brushed past the guard, for once eager to respond to
the name Sinclair. He had no idea how long he had been sleeping on the floor of the jail and at that point didn't really care.
He was just happy that someone had obviously come to his
senses and bailed him out. Maybe the world had returned to
normal. Someone was going to have to pay though. Eli and
Soley would definitely have to go and his wife was going to
have to explain the man in their bedroom who looked so much
like himself.

He made his way through the hallway as quickly as he could.

"Sinclair, you have to collect your belongings," an officer called out.

"Keep 'em," he said. "They're not mine anyway."

He wondered who had bailed him out . . . probably his wife. The guard opened the last of the doors for him and he was finally in the main entry way to the station. He immediately spotted Kyle sitting on a bench reading a paper. Although his face was covered by the pages, he recognized his brother's alligator boots.

"It's about time," he hissed as he snatched the paper from Kyle's grip.

A look of surprise came across Kyle's face but it was immediately replaced with anger. He slowly stood to his feet and opened his mouth as if to say something, then stopped upon seeing the receptionist watching them.

"Next time I'll come sooner," he said with a smile that was oddly out of place beneath his provoked eyes.

Failing to notice Kyle's reaction, Adam continued with his scolding as he turned toward the door. "I've been in there all damn day. You won't believe the shit I've been through. When I get a hold of Eli and Soley . . . " he said back to Kyle, not watching where he was going. As he burst through the swinging doors he collided with a man carrying several cups of coffee.

"Aahh!" he heard the man scream as the hot liquid flew everywhere, the empty cups plopping to the floor.

"Why don't you watch where you're going, mister?" the man said looking up at Adam.

Upon seeing the man's face, Adam was taken back, certain he could not believe what he was seeing. It was Detective Briggs: the third victim of their swamp murders.

"I, uh . . . " but the words didn't come to him.

"Yeah, well next time, please do," Briggs said before moving on past into the station. "Susie, call down and get this mess cleaned up for me, will ya'?" he asked before disappearing through a doorway.

Adam stared after him until he was out of sight. He looked at Kyle who continued out the door.

"Don't you know who that was?" he asked after they had cleared the steps of the entrance. "That was the cop you shot the other morning!"

Kyle looked at him strangely. "I don't know what you're talking about," he said before grabbing a hold of Adam's arm.

"What are you doing?" Adam demanded, Kyle's fingers digging into his arm. "Jesus Christ! There's his car," he said yanking his arm loose and pointing to the undercover car parked in front of the station.

"Come on," Kyle said roughly, pushing Adam around the corner of the station to a side street.

"Hey what are you doing? Don't you recognize his car? You said he was following you the other day," Adam begged, his heart beginning to pound.

"The only cop following me is the one you've probably sicked on me," Kyle said as he grabbed a hold of Adam and dragged him toward the Cadillac parked at the curb.

"Let go of me, Kyle," Adam said, suddenly aware that his brother seemed much stronger than himself. Oddly enough, he also felt shorter next to Kyle than he normally did.

Kyle threw him up against the side of the Cadillac, pressing his face into the window. "Shut up before I slit your throat right here in broad daylight," he threatened from behind him, keeping his voice low.

"What's going on?" Adam pleaded as Kyle yanked his arms behind his back.

"AAAHHH!" he screamed out in pain, his shoulder feeling as though it had been ripped from the socket. He turned his head and tried to wriggle loose but couldn't break Kyle's grip.

"Look buddy, if you want to live you better cooperate," Kyle warned, clamping a pair of cuffs onto one of Adam's wrists.

Adam lifted his face off of the hood of the car and started to yell, but a reflection in the window of the police station caught his eyes. In the smoked glass he could see the reflection of Kyle handcuffing him, but the person beneath Kyle was not himself. It was Charlie Sinclair. The undeniable image moved before him, as his breath left his body and his vision began to blur. He felt his knees buckle beneath him and watched himself in the body of Sinclair slide down the side of the car to the ground below. The grass before his eyes appeared ten feet tall and then faded into darkness.

A moment later he came to as his body was rolled into the trunk of the car. Kyle's image smeared into focus standing over him.

"Sorry about this Charlie boy, but I can't very well be seen driving around town with you, now can I?" he smiled before slamming the trunk. Everything instantly went dark again, only this time Adam was conscious.

* * * * *

Sergeant Hadley watched out the window of a side office as Kyle's Cadillac pulled away from the curb.

"The idiot should have talked," he said to the officer standing behind him. "Put a tail on that Cadillac. Send Briggs."

74

"Briggs?" the officer asked as if questioning the competence of the detective.

"Better send Hays, too," Hadley advised.

Chapter 10

Kyle thrust down on the horn of the Cadillac hoping to make a little headway. He had been sitting on the Crescent City Connection too long and was extremely irritated by the never ending construction on the bridge which always seemed to hold up traffic. He looked down at the Mississippi River below him, and wondered how painful the fall would be if he decided he'd had enough of waiting and decided to swim. Then the thought of the sheriff finding a man in the trunk of an abandoned car on the Mississippi Bridge brought a smile to his face.

"Oh Jesus! Come on!" he yelled as the palm of his hand hit the horn again. Finally the truck in front of him let him pass and he was once again on his way over to the West Bank. The New Orleans skyline rose up behind him, surrealistic in its towering appearance. Although it was several miles behind him, it appeared to be very close. Dark, ominous thunderheads hovered over the tall buildings, the French Quarter snuggled against the business district like a child nestled in its mother's protective arms. Even though the sun had not yet set, the dark sky hid its light beneath the blanket of clouds.

At the end of the bridge, large spatters of rain began pelting his windshield diminishing his visibility to a blur. He got onto the Expressway leading out of the city toward the wooded swamps. Almost immediately, the water began rising on the highway, but Kyle was not one to let such a ridiculous thing as hydroplaning slow him down. He pressed the gas pedal to the floor and went his usual eighty-five to ninety.

* * * * *

In the darkness, Adam could hear the rain pinging against the paint of the car. He felt as if he would smother if the hood to the trunk didn't open soon. In spite of the pouring rain, perhaps even due to its additional stifling humidity, the heat inside the trunk was unbearable. He tried to control his breathing as his mind continued to race, like it had ever since they left the station. He had been forced to accept the unacceptable. Somehow he had ended up in Charlie Sinclair's body. He had awakened that morning in Sinclair's body and everyone saw him as Sinclair. He was Sinclair.

Adam felt the car turn off the main highway onto an unpaved road. He bounced painfully around the inside of the trunk frantically searching his mind for answers that would relieve the terrible nightmare. He thought back to that morning with Monique and the child. They had been alive and so had the detective at the station. They weren't dead. Not yet, at least. He remembered the newspaper in the cab, stating it was Thursday. And how the slate card had read Thursday when they booked him. Somehow time had gone backward for him. It was three days earlier and he was now Sinclair. He thought of the Thursday he had lived three days ago and what had happened. Sinclair had come to his house in a cab and the cab driver had called the police because he thought Sinclair was trying to break into the mansion. The police had arrested him and he had sent

77

Kyle down to bail him out. Oh God. He himself. Was that him in the window? How could it be? How could any of it be?

"Okay, think, think . . . " he said aloud to himself trying to stay level headed.

He calculated that if everything was happening like it previously had on Thursday, then they were probably headed toward the Barataria area.

Just then Adam felt the car come to a halt, the momentum sliding his body into the crowbar behind his back. Kyle was never light on the brakes and this was certainly no exception.

He heard the engine cut off, and the car swayed as Kyle got out. He heard people's voices and strained to hear what they were saying, but from inside the trunk they gargled into a murmur.

Terrified of what lay outside the car, Adam tried to recreate the situation in his mind. He remembered with a chill, that he was the one who had opened the trunk with Sinclair inside. There's no way that will happen, he told himself.

His heart stopped as he could hear a set of keys jingling ever closer. One was inserted into the keyhole of the trunk and the lid slowly creaked open.

As light and rain spilled through the opening trunk, Adam recognized the charcoal gray suit that was slowly revealed before him. Just as he realized that what he had dreaded was coming true, the trunk cleared the face of himself—Claiborne—standing before him. The rain poured down his dark hair, streaking across his handsome face. His piercing green eyes stared down upon him.

"Enjoy the ride?" the familiar yet eerily removed voice asked.

Adam stared up at himself in speechless terror. He was on the receiving end of his own cold ungiving stare. The stare that represented fear and weakness, masked by evil, was now directed toward him. He wanted to say something, anything to let Claiborne know, but no words would enter his mouth. He knew he could never convince himself of such a distorted reality.

"Get out," Claiborne said quietly before stepping away from the trunk.

But Adam couldn't move.

"Didn't you hear what he said, dip shit?" Kyle goaded from a few feet back. "Get out."

Adam knew what was coming, and even though he didn't want to face it, he knew he had no other choice.

Claiborne, Kyle, and Marshal stood back and watched as Adam sat up and began struggling to get out of the car, his hands still cuffed behind his back. He awkwardly managed to work his way out and just as his feet touched the wet ground, he was greeted by a fist to the stomach, the fist belonging to Claiborne.

As Adam doubled over in pain, he heard an approaching car come to a splashing halt right next to him and the other men. He looked up to see Monique get out of her old Ford and run toward him.

"Charlie!" she cried, but Kyle grabbed her by the waist.

"Hold on there, darling," Kyle said. "We're glad you could make it, but you're just supposed to watch."

Just as Adam straightened from a crouched position, he saw Claiborne come menacingly toward him again. His head flew back in excruciating pain as Claiborne's fist connected with his jaw. His eyes passed across the overhanging trees, his vision momentarily blurred from his watering tear ducts. He tried with all his might to bring his head back down, only to be met by Claiborne's angry face.

"I told you, never, ever, come to my house!" Claiborne yelled, before pounding him in the face again.

79

Once again Adam saw the trees overhead, his ears beginning to ring in a piercing pitch. His head bobbed sloppily forward and he heard Monique screaming.

"Charlie!"

"Now you've involved the cops," Claiborne said into his eyes before hitting him again.

"Were you coming to bring him the money?" he heard Kyle yell.

He felt another blow to the face, but wasn't sure where it came from. No longer able to hold his head up, he went crashing to the soggy ground. Through a haze he could see the shiny leather shoes his wife had bought him for Christmas, muddy water dancing off their smooth surface.

He struggled to lift his head and he saw Monique still fighting with Kyle.

"We'll have it tonight," she promised. "Leave him alone!"

"Tonight then," he heard Claiborne say, before the shiny shoe lifted and swiftly kicked him in the face.

* * * * *

"Holy shit, they're going to kill the guy," Briggs whispered to his partner from behind a cypress stump. He and Hays had been hard put to keep up with Kyle in the pouring rain, several times narrowly missing an accident. Somehow, though, they had managed not to lose the speeding Cadillac and had followed it out to the bayou.

The two detectives had parked their car down the road and gone by foot into the clearing where the Cadillac and Lincoln were parked. They positioned themselves behind some trees,

80

far enough away from the parked cars as not to be seen, yet they could still see what was happening. Just when the encroaching night threatened to steal the scene from their sight, the beating ended.

"It looks like they're done," Detective Hays observed. "Let's get out of here so we have enough of a head start on the Cadillac."

"But the guy looks like he's dead," Briggs argued.

"Hey, our orders were to follow the Cadillac and not interfere. Now come on, or we could be dead," Hays insisted before turning back in the direction of their car.

Briggs immediately complied with his partner's wishes, not wanting to be deserted in the dark woods with the possibility of facing the Claiborne brothers and Marshal Long on his own. He followed in the direction of Hays through the thick cypress trees, running as fast as he could to keep up with his athletically superior partner. Suddenly, as he ran past a tree, his sleeve caught on an errant branch and the momentum ripped open his shirt.

"Son-of-a-bitch," he howled, grabbing his arm in pain.

"Come on," Hays ordered from in front of him.

Briggs held his injured arm as they made their way to the road where his car was parked. He pulled the keys from his pocket and as he got into the driver's side, he looked down at his scraped skin.

"Shit! I lost my watch," he exclaimed.

"Well it's too late now," Hays said.

Briggs started the engine, but wasn't sure in which direction to move the car. Hays noticed his hesitation.

"Pull down over there," he said pointing to a path that looked as if it used to be a road, no more than a hundred years ago.

Briggs quickly obliged, groaning at the sound of his muffler dragging on the underbrush.

Moments later, Adam's Lincoln turned onto the main road where the undercover car had been only seconds earlier. Kyle's Cadillac followed behind it and both cars passed. Briggs instantly started the engine and slowly pulled out to follow.

* * * * *

Although Adam was lying face down in the mud, the pain was too unbearable to even attempt to move. He couldn't tell where his skin ended and the ground began, it all pulsated into one bloody mess. The downpour had ceased, the rain no longer pelting his back. All was dark and silent, except for his own breathing and the wild, eerie chatter of the swampland, preparing for the impending night.

He felt beaten beyond repair, and didn't see the point in getting up just yet. Maybe if he lay there long enough, his world would return to its old self. Thinking he was alone, he was surprised when a gentle hand caressed his hair.

"Charlie?" he heard Monique ask softly. She took hold of his side and slowly rolled him over.

Everything ached, burned and throbbed. There were so many sharp jabs coming from his rib cage he thought for sure he must have broken at least one bone. Trying to control the overpowering pain, he remembered to breathe again. He turned his head slightly, and looked up at Monique.

She was looking at him with such love in her bright green eyes, her golden hair darkened from the rain. Tears streamed down her face, but she wiped them away with a swift movement of her hand. Even though it was steaming outside, he could see that she was covered in chills, her clothes soaked from the downpour, her strong beautiful face appearing so sad.

"Aren't you a sight," she said with a bittersweet smile, forcing the tears back down. "Can you make it to the car?"

Adam turned his eyes to the left and saw the wheels of the old Ford. Although it was only a few feet away, he shuddered at the thought of having to get up off the ground.

"Come on," she said, putting her hands under his arms. As she lifted him into an upright seated position, he felt something trickling down his face, his left eye feeling strangely numb. When Monique saw his face in full view she winced as if taken aback by the sight.

"Those bastards," she said hotly under her breath, inspecting Adam like a tiger protecting her cub. "We'll have Wilton fix you up."

She helped him to his feet and he hobbled to the old Ford. He leaned against the side of the car as she creaked open the heavy door which let out a wail.

Adam was silent as he allowed himself to be lowered into the seat by the fresh smelling woman before him. Not sure what else to do, he complied like a child in the hands of a warm understanding mother.

She knelt down beside him and removed her blouse, leaving her shivering torso bare except for a burgundy colored bra. Her shaking hands held the shirt out to him.

"Put this against your eye to stop the bleeding," she instructed before shutting the car door and rushing around to the driver's side. She reached into the back seat and pulled out a faded old jean vest and quickly put it on before getting in and starting the engine.

* * * * *

The musty smell of the old Ford reminded Adam of the car his father used to drive, the old springs of the seat pressing against his legs like skeletons trying to escape the threadbare upholstery. As the car began to move forward, a chorus of rattling burst into play, as if piece by piece the vehicle would decompose, each freed component whirling in its own direction.

He took the blood soaked blouse away from his eye and pulled down the visor, revealing a mirror on its underside. He stared motionlessly at the image before him. He had never really noticed Sinclair's face before and now that it was staring back at him so pathetically, blood oozing from the cut above his brow, he noticed for the first time how much older the face was than he had thought. Funny how he had always thought of Sinclair as an irresponsible kid no more than twenty-one or so, but upon closer inspection, he saw that he was probably in his late twenties. He raised his hand to the bleeding brow and touched his fingertips to the ruby red blood.

"It's going to need stitches," Monique said.

He looked over at Monique, thinking how willingly she had accepted him as if he were her husband. He was an invader in her world, a Peeping Tom welcomed with open arms.

He noticed his unfamiliar arms, attached to him like hideously strange appendages. How had he gone the whole day without seeing them and recognizing them to be someone else's? They were the thin, tanned arms of a man much weaker than himself.

Suddenly a rush came over Adam, and the panic returned. He was trapped. Trapped!

He looked out the dirty windshield as they rounded the corner of the road and pulled out onto the two-lane highway. The long beams of the headlights cut through the darkness like a knife, momentarily illuminating the otherwise invisible night world of the scattering blue and red dragonflies and mosquitoes gorged with blood.

* * * * *

Monique looked wearily over at her husband. Something was wrong. Deadly wrong. His movements were so different. That morning he had terrified her with his strange behavior.

"Charlie, tell me what's going on," she said.

He didn't answer, only continued to stare ahead. She had never seen him so cold and distant before. After a moment, she turned her eyes back to the highway.

"I don't understand why you went to Claiborne's house. It didn't accomplish anything. All it did was piss him off. Besides, I told you Wilton was going to give me some money tonight to help pay off the loan," she said in a tone that was mildly reprimanding.

Adam was silent as he continued to watch the fleeting highway pass under the hood of the car. He refused to be forced into following through with another man's life. He had his own and was intent on getting it back.

He felt Monique's eyes upon him. How could he possibly tell her that he was an impostor? He met her eyes briefly, then quickly looked away.

Monique shuddered as a chill ran through her body. "Charlie?" she whispered, feeling as though he were a stranger. But he didn't answer, he just continued to stare ahead.

She spoke quietly and uncertainly, almost in a whisper. "I was worried to death about you. I didn't know what had happened. I didn't know what to think. Finally, around six o'clock, I got a call at work from Claiborne saying they were taking you out to Jefferson Parish. I thought for sure they were going to kill you."

It was clear that he had no intentions of talking to her. Her husband was normally the most open and warm person she knew; never before had he shut her out so completely. Unable to bear the feeling it gave her, she tried to think of other things.

They both stared ahead in silence as the city lights drew nearer. Adam was tired but he had to keep thinking. He had to come up with some answers.

He looked down at the lights of Algiers, the area in which he had grown up. Although he hadn't been back for years, he was forced to pass by it every time he went to the West Bank.

As they made their way toward the Crescent City Connection, he stared down at the familiar buildings passing by. The reflection of Sinclair in the window watched over the ride like a ghost.

If he went back now, they surely wouldn't recognize him, he thought, a pain instantly hitting his soul, catching him off guard against the past. He longed to see his mother for a moment, for just a single moment. Then he quickly pushed the idea from his mind, reminding himself that he never truly had a mother. A real mother that is. A mother who loved him and protected him. Even though his father was the physically abusive one, he blamed his mother just as much for the pain he and Kyle endured. She lived in the land where men ruled and women submitted even at the expense of their children. She would sit silently by while his father beat them for something as minor as spilling a glass of water. Although she was an intelligent woman and could have successfully supported herself and the children on her own, she chose not to. Instead, she remained chained to the torture with the rest of them and Adam hated her for it.

Their mother was the deepest source of friction between the two brothers. Kyle believed her to be in the same category as the Virgin Mary, suffering through her hardships with the pristine honor of a saint. Yet, in spite of his devotion to her, upon his frequent visits home, he was nearly as abusive to her as their father was. He adored her with such love, yet abused her as if she were worthless. He always repented immediately, begging for forgiveness and promising reformation, but somehow he always managed once again to hurt her. To Adam, the whole situation was perverted and just the mere thought of it felt like a huge black cloud bearing down upon him: one that sometimes took days to shake.

He struggled to return his thoughts to the present, as the car rose over the bridge. They must be headed toward the French Quarter, he thought. Even though he saw no point in going to Monique's home, to Sinclair's home, he had no idea where else to go.

Chapter 11

They drove on in silence, as the old Ford rattled off of Camp Street and headed in the direction of the French Quarter. Monique reached over in front of Adam and flipped open the glove box.

"Time for music," she said, anything to break the silence.

As she rummaged through the cluttered compartment, Adam was struck by the beauty of her long slender arm, so smooth, porcelain, and graceful. As she moved in front of him, he noticed how a strand of wet hair curled across her neck and lightly touched the top of her chest. Without warning, a dark, but highly erotic feeling crept through him. He was instantly back in the previous night's dream, staring down at the body of Monique. She lay in the bottom of the cellar looking so beautiful, her long hair dancing in the water. Adam turned his eyes to the passenger window to escape the guilty feeling that overtook him. Monique popped a cassette into the player, and the Neville Brothers' Yellow Moon floated through the car speakers.

Although Adam stared intently out at the passing old buildings of the Quarter, the images of the haunting dream rushed relentlessly at him.

He stood over the pit, with the lantern in hand, as her lovely eyes had slowly opened and looked up at him from the dead.

A smile worked its way across her pale lips and she spoke the words . . . "Father Jacob said you'd be back." Suddenly the words jolted through him like lightning. She was standing naked in front of him, her lips grazing his ear, then whispering . . . "Give me back my life." He remembered the feeling of surrender as he wrapped her in his arms and made love to her.

"Oh Jesus," he said aloud and raised his hand to his brow. "I let this happen," he uttered looking toward Monique who was watching him closely.

"How do you know Father Jacob?" he managed to ask.

Monique heard the voice, struck by the unfamiliarly smooth texture of it, void of the usual stammers and stutters. His eyes looked frightened and distant even though they were staring straight at her. Baffled not only by his voice, but by the strange question it carried, she hesitated a moment. "Who?" she asked uncertainly.

"Father Jacob. In my dream. He told you I'd be back," he said as if trying to control the panic.

"I don't know any priests," Monique said, looking at him strangely.

Adam's mind whirled back to the day of his confession, the priest standing before him refusing to forgive him. Like a blast of cold air, the Father's words came rushing into his mind . . . Until you know the sorrow of your victims, your sins cannot be forgiven . . . "Until you know the sorrow of your victims," Adam said aloud recounting the condemning sentence. Could it have been the priest that did this to him, by bestowing a penance upon him after all? A penance of making him his own victim!

"Father, what have you done?" he exclaimed then turned to Monique as if she had been hearing his thoughts. "I've got to get to the church."

"What?" she asked in confusion.

"Take me to St. Mary's Cathedral," he said urgently, looking about the streets to get his bearings.

"Why?"

"Take a left!" he exclaimed, but she continued to stare at him blankly.

"Take a left!" he shouted, grabbing the wheel.

The car swerved violently to the left and Monique screamed as the shrill, blaring horn of another car screeched past.

"Let go! I'm going to wreck!" she wailed, struggling to regain control of the wayward car. Another car whirled past along the narrow one way street, barely missing the front of their car. Monique slammed her foot on the brake just in time to avoid plowing down a frightened looking elderly couple standing on the curb.

After the car came to a violently sudden stop, Monique looked over at Adam as if he had lost his mind. Not willing to waste a moment, he didn't take time to explain. He had to find the priest as soon as possible so he could stop the hellish nightmare.

A small group of pedestrians looked at him strangely as he bolted from the car. They were on the outskirts of the French Quarter, only a few blocks away from St. Mary's Cathedral, where the offending priest resided. He took out running in the direction of the church, no longer feeling his painfully bruised body.

* * * * *

The dark night flew past Adam as he ran as fast as he could

toward the church. With every step, his feet jammed against the hard pavement that was interspersed with brick and cobblestone. The faint sound of the lively bands on Bourbon Street floated eerily through the dark, abandoned streets that formed the outer-lying area of the French Quarter. The sad notes were soon replaced by the sound of his own heavy breathing and of the clicking of his ever slowing pace. His side began to ache, and his eyes began to sting from the sweat that had traveled down from his forehead.

"Damn it," he scowled as he was forced to give in to the need to stop for breath. His own body was in excellent shape, obeying his every command, therefore he found it hard to tolerate the weaker body he now inhabited. He stood bent over gasping for air when he felt the presence of someone staring at him. He looked up to see a frightened old homeless man standing in the shadows of a doorway, watching him as if he were a potential attacker. Suddenly, the man was lit up by the headlights of a car turning onto the narrow street. Adam looked to see the Ford coming toward him slowly. The old man disappeared into the shadows as Adam turned back and continued his way toward the church.

"Charlie!" Monique's voice echoed down the street, almost drowned out by the rattling of the old car.

In spite of her beckoning calls, he kept up at a steady pace. After another block, he was relieved to see the cathedral within sight. Like his mansion, it had always represented safety to him, a place where the outside world dare not tread.

He quickly mounted the stone stairs that led up to the large wooden doors. He pulled at the rusted handle but the doors didn't budge, they were locked. Anger welled up in his chest at the thought of the priest on the other side taunting him with the locked door.

"Open up," he commanded as he pounded his fists against the splintery wood.

Monique pulled up in her car, sending lights streaking across the front of the cathedral.

"Open up, Father Jacob," he wailed. A sharp pain jetted through his hand. "Damn," he hissed upon seeing the rotted wood embedded in his palm. Sweat ran down his face as he stepped back from the entrance to search for another door. Suddenly, a feeling of vertigo threw him off balance, and the cathedral took on an ominous appearance as it rose up from the ground, towering over him. He was struck by the foreboding darkness it possessed. The gargoyles seemed to jump out at him from above, daunting him not to enter. He stumbled back from the entrance and looked around to the side wall which disappeared into darkness. He spotted a small narrow door chiseled into the stone and quickly grabbed the handle.

"Charlie!" cried Monique upon seeing Adam race around to the side of the unfamiliar cathedral. She began running toward him, but before she could reach him, he disappeared through the door.

After a slight hesitation, she entered the cathedral, following in Adam's path down an entryway that led to the main sanctuary. She felt like an intruder stepping into a world where she had no business. She believed in spirits and saints and such, but the Catholic Church had always seemed so menacing and foreign to her. Terrified of her husband's strange actions, she had to follow. Moments behind him, she walked as if she were in enemy territory down the long, dimly lit hallway. The space was so narrow that she felt that the slightest movement of the walls would crush them like ants. Quickening her pace, she followed him out into the empty cathedral toward a looming altar. A large cross of an agonized Jesus hung above the altar staring down at her as if he were a prisoner begging to be set free.

"Father Jacob," Adam called out, his voice ringing through the structure, echoing back and forth.

"Jacob what have you done to me?" he cried out.

Suddenly, an old woman's voice crackled from behind him. "Young man you are in a place of worship," she scolded.

Adam and Monique were both startled by the unexpected presence of someone in the back of the church and they swung around to see where the voice was coming from. Shuffling footsteps hissed across the marble floor, as a small, fragile old nun stepped out of the darkness into the light of the votive candles burning beneath the statues. Adam instantly recognized her to be Sister Clara; the nun who had helped him to cling ever so tightly to the church after he had left home, nearly twenty years ago. She hobbled toward him with the help of a cane to steady herself.

"Sister Clara, is Father Jacob here?" he impatiently asked.

The nun looked up at him curiously. "Do I know you?" she asked, studying his frazzled face.

"It's Adam Clai . . . " but he caught himself. "You advised me once. Have you seen the replacement for Father Paul. His name is Father Jacob."

"Father Paul hasn't been replaced," she said with a smile as if finding the notion amusing.

"He's not dead?" Adam asked.

"Why no child. He's in the back office writing tomorrow's sermon," she said.

Of course, he thought. It was two days earlier than the time he had confessed, so it was possible that Father Paul wasn't dead yet! The thought of Father Paul still living shone out to him like a buoy to a drowning man. He could reconfess his sins and Father Paul could absolve him, lifting the unjust penance Father Jacob had inflicted upon him.

"Thank you, Sister," he exclaimed, then abruptly turned and ran back down the hall he and Monique had come up.

"Charlie?!" Monique exclaimed, starting after him.

* * * * *

Adam swung open the door to the office where he had often spoken to Father Paul in private.

"Father Paul," he began but staggered back upon seeing what awaited him.

Monique saw Adam's stunned reaction and quickly came up to his side, looking into the room. The dead bluish body of a middle-aged priest was seated upright at a desk in a dark leather chair. His eyes were open and glassed over, life having abruptly abandoned them, freezing them in a bloodcurdling stare.

The dead man's eyes pierced into Monique, seizing her very soul. Waves of terror ripped through her, gripping her stomach in a stronghold. She put her hand over her mouth and stepped back from the room.

"How did you know?" she gasped, looking at Adam in amazement. "Do you know this man?!"

Adam lunged forward into the warmly lit room, and grabbed the priest and began shaking him as if to wake him.

"You've got to help me," he begged.

Monique watched in horror as Adam frantically pulled at the priest.

"He's dead!" she shouted, but Adam continued to shake him.

94

"Oh Jesus God, PLEASE!   Get up!" he commanded the dead man.

"He's DEAD!" Monique screamed, taking a hold of Adam's arm.

Upon finally hearing Monique's words, Adam released the priest and stepped back, his eyes still fixed on the dead body as it slumped down onto the desk.

He turned away with his hands to his face, trying to fight back the panic.   He paced about the room like a caged animal.   He wiped his forehead.   He tried to calm himself, to tell himself that everything would be okay.   Tears began streaming down his face.   He had been condemned to hell.   The church he had grown to trust had turned on him, siding with the horror which had always plagued him.   The walls seemed to laugh out at him and the saints goaded from their pedestals.   He had to escape, to get away from it all where he could think more clearly.

Monique watched him with guarded eyes as he moved about the room.   Something was deathly wrong.   His face was red and streaked with tears, raw terror surrounding him.   Although he looked like her husband, his speech and demeanor were completely different as if someone else inhabited the frantic flesh.   She wanted to say something, anything, but didn't know what.   Suddenly, her attention was caught by the swishing sound of the nun's flowing habit and the clicking of her cane as she made her way down the hallway toward the open office.   She looked down at the dead priest and wondered what the nun would think.   Her husband had said he was dead before they even saw him.   Perhaps the nun would think they had something to do with it.

"What do we do?" she asked, only to find that her hus-

95

band was no longer in the room with her. She was alone in the lurid place with a dead priest at her side. She lunged for the door.

* * * * *

At a fast gait, Adam passed along the outer dark wall of the cathedral. Even the moon had been snatched from the sky by the dark forces, leaving the night completely black. He would go to a restaurant, somewhere with a brightly lit room, where he could examine the facts in a clearer light.

Every muscle in his body was tense, and he once again began to feel the pain he had been dealt. Although he no longer felt any streaming blood, his eye was throbbing.

Monique burst through the side door of the cathedral. "Charlie!" she screamed upon spotting Adam moving along the stone wall. "Stop!"

To her frustration, he kept going, so lost in his own thoughts that he didn't even hear her. She ran with all her might to catch up with him and upon reaching him, she grabbed him forcefully by the arm. "Damn it, stop! I can't chase you anymore," she wailed swinging him around to face her. His unfamiliar eyes looked so strangely at her, then he turned away again.

"Charlie?" she cried, desperate to get through to him.

Jealousy and anger rose in Adam's chest. How could she not see who he was? How could she still be so blind as to think he was her husband?

He swung around on her and the look of confusion on her face fed his anger even more. Frightened, she turned to run, to get away from his hideous expression, but he grabbed her wrist, pulling her back with his forceful grip.

"Can't you see that I'm not your damn husband?" he spewed in a low guttural voice, looking deeply into her eyes.

Monique fell back, stunned by the determination emanating from the man before her. The darkness began closing in on her as she looked into his searching, unfamiliar eyes.

Suddenly, he grabbed her mouth with his hand and passionately and forcefully kissed her. "Is that how your Charlie kisses?" he demanded as he shoved her against the cold, hard wall.

With her heart racing, Monique tried to pull away from his grip, but he pressed his body heavily against hers and ran his hand up her thigh. She was breathless as he pressed his lips to her ear. "Recognize the touch?" he whispered. It was her husband's hand moving over her, but it was so different, so deliberate.

Panic overcame her and she struggled to get free.

"Let me go," she cried, the heat of his body pressing tighter against hers.

"You came to me for a loan," he whispered, his hand continuing its course up her skirt, stroking her thigh. "You had no collateral so you offered yourself," he said softly. "Did you tell your husband what you did for the money?"

Her head fell back, his fluid, hypnotic voice taking hold. "My baby was sick," she cried, the black caving in on her.

He pushed her tighter against the wall. "How was it, now?" he asked, forcefully spreading her legs and pulling her up around him. "First we were against the wall," he whispered, pulling her vest open to reveal her bra underneath. "Then the dress," he continued, putting his hand inside the lace and cupping her breast in his hand.

97

Her breathing became heavy as she yielded to the pleasure. "That's it," he said softly.

Although unwilling, she was moved by his powerful touch. A touch that she'd only known from one man and in the darkness that man appeared. It was Adam Claiborne resting against her, speaking into her soul. Her mind shot back to the day she'd had sex with Claiborne. Not wanting to play the victim, she had forced herself to enjoy his touch, only to be sucked in by it.

He ran his lips along her neck.

"Remember how I made you come even though you resisted?"

The sensuous words turned to arrogance as they slithered along her ear. Humiliation overcame her as she remembered that she truly had been carried away with her attraction to the ruthless Claiborne. Anger rose in her like a vicious animal, devouring her pride with one fatal lunge. "You bastard!" she screamed as she shoved him away with all her might.

She was beating him in the face and the stomach, lunging with everything she had in a rampant fury.

"You prick! Did you think I was going to let you take something from me?! I took from you!" she bellowed, desperately trying to erase him with her fists. She pounded and pounded until the flesh gave way. Suddenly, she realized that he wasn't fighting her, only standing there taking her blows without defending himself. She pulled back, sickened by the wetness on her skin. Her shaking hands were covered by what appeared in the shadows to be black ink, but by the warmth of it, she knew it was blood. She looked up to the cut above his eye, once again bleeding profusely.

"What have I done?" she whispered, as the two looked at one another. Adam turned away, ashamed of his attraction to her even then.

Monique looked down at the blood on her hands and back up at Adam. He looked like her husband, but for a moment, she was speaking to Adam Claiborne.

"I woke up in bed with you this morning, but I'm not your husband," he said bitterly.

She stared at him closely, trying to see what she had heard moments earlier. "This isn't possible."

"Isn't it?" he asked, turning to face her.

She watched his face move in and out of the shadows. The same features that once belonged to her husband had taken on a completely different look. The face which had once been so innocent and meek had transformed into a man with anger and fear. It was Adam Claiborne without mistake.

"Adam?" she whispered, trying desperately to grasp the freakish situation. "How . . . how did this happen?" she asked, her voice barely audible.

"A priest did it to me," he answered assuredly. "The priest that replaces the dead one inside."

The gnawing sight of the dead priest flashed through her mind. "Why?" she asked.

"I killed you and your husband," he replied, then waited for her response, but there was none, only a dazed look of disbelief. "The day after," he continued slowly, "I went to confession and the priest refused to absolve me of my sins. Apparently, he didn't like my reasons. The next morning I woke up in bed with you, only it wasn't the next morning. Somehow, the bastard sent me back in time, from Sunday to Thursday."

"But you're in Charlie's body," she said.

Adam held out his arms with a sardonic smile. "I guess he thought I needed a new perspective on the situation."

"If you're Adam Claiborne, then who just beat you up in the swamp?"

Adam shook his head, unable to believe it himself. "Me," then the smile faded as he turned his eyes upon her. "In thirty-six hours we're both going to be dead. I know, because I'm the one who kills us."

Monique leaned against the stone wall feeling weak and terrified. Her mind heard one thing but her eyes saw another. She had heard of spirits splitting and taking on new faces, traveling from one body to the next, but that had been only a tale told to her by the man who raised her. Something that was far removed and only happened in the forbidden practice of black magic more than a hundred years ago. A chill ran down her spine as she felt the presence of the cathedral behind her. She was still on unfamiliar soil, now being forced to believe the impossible. She looked up at Adam who stood watching her.

"You kill me and Charlie?" she asked as if suddenly hearing his words and finding them as hard to comprehend as the thought of Adam being inside of her husband's body.

"Yes," he replied.

A look of contempt came across her soft face. "But I'm going to pay off your loan tonight," she said.

"Well, you don't. You only pay a small portion of it."

"So you kill us?" she asked, unable to believe it.

Adam looked at her squarely. "Even though you betrayed me, I didn't mean to kill you."

"Gee, that makes me feel better. How about Charlie? Did you mean to kill him?" she asked

"Yes," he replied simply. "He stole money from me."

"Charlie never stole a cent in his life," she rivaled. "You're a bastard, you know that?"

"And what does that make your Charlie?" Adam demanded, his anger rising. "An ungrateful slimebag who steals from someone who tries to help him?!"

"If your reasons for killing are so righteous, why the hell didn't your priest forgive you? Why did he think you needed a new perspective on the situation? Could it be that you have a warped sense of justice?"

His head was pounding with anger and he wanted to strike back, but he had no response to her questions. He didn't have the answers. All he knew was that he had reasons for all of his decisions.

Monique saw his silence and the thoughts behind it. "If what you say is true and Charlie really did steal from you, then I guess now that you're in his body you can put things straight, right? Then there shouldn't be any killings."

Adam thought for a moment in silence. "That's right," he said, somewhat relieved by the idea. Maybe that was the purpose of the whole ordeal, for him to set things straight.

His response seemed to turn her stomach, as she looked at him in disgust. "As if stealing was worth killing over," she said, then turned toward her car.

As Adam silently watched her walking away, his hate for Charlie surged up inside of him again. He had tried to help him and he had spit it all back in his face. Now he was the one suffering and for what? A low life bastard who probably had a drug problem.

Suddenly the piercing sound of a siren echoed down the streets.

"Come on!" Monique called to him, waving from the car, but he didn't move. He didn't know what to do. He was angry at her, and at the whole unjust situation. "Where else have you got to go?" she called.

As they drove off toward the French Quarter, an ambulance pulled up to the cathedral.

101

Chapter 12

Detective Briggs sat stewing behind the wheel of the undercover cop car parked alongside the sparsely lit street of Carondelet. Unable to believe that he had lost a watch that had been in the family for years, he stared down at the white stripe on his otherwise tanned arm.

Hays noticed Briggs's dismay, and felt a slight pang of guilt for not letting him go back to retrieve it from the branch that had ripped it from his partner's arm.

"Look Briggs, if you had backtracked, we would have lost these guys for sure," he said, pointing to Kyle's Cadillac which was halfway up the block, parked in front of an old apartment building. "We've barely been able to keep up with them as it is," he argued.

The two detectives had been tailing the Cadillac ever since it had left the swamps of the West Bank almost two hours earlier. It had made periodic stops in various neighborhoods along the way, sometimes at businesses, other times at houses or apartment buildings. They had waited in the shadows, parked several hundred feet back from the Cadillac, watching as Kyle went into the establishments. Almost without fail, Kyle was the one who went inside, while Marshal waited in the passenger's seat. Only occasionally did Marshal lug his big body out of the car to accompany his boss.

The detectives had been forced to keep an unusually far distance between themselves and the suspects, because of the Cadillac's frequent, sudden stops. Hays had incessantly nagged the less cautious Briggs about not getting too close and was feeling guilty about that as well as the loss of the watch.

"You can go back for it when we get off duty," Hays said with slight irritation.

"Whenever that is," Briggs groaned, imagining the precious antique lodged in the belly of an alligator.

"Oh Christ," Hays mumbled. He wanted to tell his partner to stop sniveling, but refrained.

Just then, the detectives saw the front door to the apartment building swing open.

"Here we go," Briggs said, spotting Kyle, who was exiting the dilapidated structure and heading for the Cadillac.

Kyle opened the door to the driver's side and threw a record book onto the seat beside Marshal, who was one step away from snoozing.

"Wake up, fat boy," he goaded as he plopped down behind the wheel. He started the engine and put the car in reverse, looking over at Marshal's languid face.

"Hang on," he said with a smile, then rammed his foot onto the gas.

The Cadillac tore out in a fury, but instead of going forward, it sailed backward.

Briggs, who had already started his engine in preparation to follow the Cadillac, was thrown off guard by the backing vehicle that was rapidly approaching them. "What's he doing?" he asked in a slight panic.

Continuing to gain speed of over thirty miles an hour, the shiny Cadillac headed straight for the front of their brown car.

"He's going to hit us!" Briggs cried at the intimidating sight of the advancing bumper. He fumbled with the gear shift, not sure whether to go into reverse or forward to avoid the seemingly inevitable collision.

Moments before the two cars met, the Cadillac swerved to the side and came to rest, right beside the unmarked car. Kyle leaned forward, looking into the driver's window at Briggs and Hays.

"Good evening, gentlemen," he greeted with a devious smile and a tip of his head. "I was wondering if you knew how to get to the South Ward."

The two detectives looked at each other, shaken by the strange turn of events. "Does he really want directions?" Briggs whispered to Hays.

"How the hell am I supposed to know?"

Briggs looked back up at the smiling Kyle and his lethargic accomplice. "Uh, yeah, uh . . . you take the—"

"I tell you what," Kyle interrupted, looking genuinely at Briggs. "Since you know the way, why don't we follow you instead of you following us?"

Briggs felt his face grow hot as the blood rushed to his head like an over-gorged tick ready to pop. "We're not following you," he said as convincingly as he could muster.

A frown of disappointment replaced Kyle's perverse smile. "Ah, shucks, and I was looking forward to that high speed chase," and with that, Kyle's foot bore down on the accelerator. Sizzling tires smoked on the pavement, the wheels reeling round and round, before traction finally took hold. The Cadillac tore out in a blaze leaving in its wake a foul stench of burning rubber. Stunned by their own level of stupidity, Briggs and Hays looked on in disbelief as the Cadillac raced away from them.

"Get going!" Hays shouted at Briggs whose hands had turned to two huge baseball mitts that fumbled to maneuver the lever to drive. It went from reverse to neutral to reverse. "What the hell are you waiting on?"

Finally, Briggs lodged it into drive and they tore out in pursuit of the escaping Cadillac that was nearly out of sight.

"Take a right," Hays instructed in a shout.

The car swayed to the side as they ignored the stop sign, turning violently onto Howard Avenue. Briggs thought of his left front tire which was completely bald and prayed it passed the strenuous test.

At the sight of the approaching intersection, Hays shook his head, "I don't believe this!" It was Lee Circle, a frustrating intersection in the European tradition of a round-about that took the place of a traffic light. A bronze General Lee stood in the center of the merry-go-round for cars like an incompetent traffic cop guiding them in every which wrong direction. As they pulled up to the intersection, it was impossible to see which of the several choices put before them was the path the Cadillac had taken.

"Well, go on," Hays impatiently instructed.

Briggs pulled out into the circle and as they passed each exit, they peered down the street for any sign of the Cadillac before continuing around to the next. Upon full completion of the intersection, Hays slammed his fist against the dashboard. "Shit!" he screamed as he put his head into his hands.

At the sight of the perplexed detectives, Kyle broke out into laughter. "And to think those bumbling idiots are supposed to protect and serve," he said to Marshal who sat quietly relishing his boss' sense of humor.

Kyle pulled his Cadillac out from behind a parked car where they had been hiding in the dark, watching Briggs complete the circle of the intersection. Keeping their lights off, they stole away in the opposite direction.

Chapter 13

Adam watched Monique as she maneuvered the old car through the narrow streets that formed a dark web around the outskirts of the French Quarter. Although he was still angry, something she had mentioned took the edge off of his resentment. "You said something about having a sick baby?" he asked.

"My daughter has acute asthma," she answered without taking her eyes off of the road.

"Why didn't you tell me you needed the loan for your child?" he asked. "I wouldn't even have hesitated to give it to you."

"I didn't want your pity."

"But, you let me —"

"Adam . . . " she said sharply, her green eyes flashing toward him. "I guess I should call you Adam. You look on my class as poor white trash. Leeches sucking on the bellies of the rich. Am I right?"

Adam looked at her silently, her beautiful eyes appearing so strong and piercing as if reading his soul. He turned his eyes away. "Yes," he replied.

Monique sighed, then looked back to the street. "I may be poor, but I'm not a parasite," she said. "And I certainly don't want your pity."

106

* * * * *

As they approached the heart of the French Quarter, the usual hustle and bustle of the night partiers came alive. Monique pulled the car up to the intersection of Bourbon and Dumaine, and with some difficulty, began crossing Bourbon. The sea of intoxicated pedestrians with cups of beer, Daiquiries, and the local Hurricane drink, slowly parted for the noisy, smoking car, like a herd of senseless cattle unaware they were making way for an intruder.

Adam watched the drunken, droopy-eyed partiers with disdain. Although many were tourists, it was the locals he couldn't forgive. He truly did think of them as vermin, nibbling on the very backbone of society: too lazy to work but not too lazy to party. Monique had been accurate in her assessment of how he viewed the lower class of the populace, but what she hadn't known was that his slanted outlook had been inadvertently formed by his father. He was a tall wiry man with a temper that led him from one public brawl to another. He used to hang out along the lively Bourbon Street, leaving home in the evening and not returning until the wee hours of the morning, always arriving with the stench of booze and sometimes reeking of worse. He was a lazy man with absolutely no qualms about living off the government; it was his God-given right as an American citizen. In the eighteen years Adam had lived with him, he never once saw him work, not even so much as to wash his own dirty underwear when his wife was ill. When Adam left home, he was determined not to follow in his father's footsteps. He did everything he could to transcend the shackles of poverty and with his escape, he brought with him a jaded distrust of the entire class. The

French Quarter—especially Bourbon Street—seemed to attract that class, so Adam simply avoided it. To him it was a foul, disgusting place of gluttony and shame, where every staggering drunk reminded him of the past.

After crossing the noisy street, Monique and Adam continued their way down Dumaine for a couple of blocks, where the lights and noise diminished tremendously. The only signs of life were a few people strewn out along the block, some in couples, others alone. Monique pulled the car up to the curb in front of a small bar with a blinking neon sign hanging overhead that read . . . "Jimmy Blues".

Adam knew the place. Over a year ago he had visited the nightclub to set up a loan to the owner, Jimmy Brown. That night was the first time Adam had laid eyes upon Monique. While waiting for Jimmy, he had taken a seat in the back of the club just as she came out to do her first set. Through the darkness he had watched her as she mesmerized the packed audience with her singing. Ten months later, when she called to see him about a loan, he instantly remembered her; he had never forgotten her. He knew the moment he heard her voice that she was the same beauty he had so attentively watched from the shadows. Even after they shared the intimacy of sex, he never confided to her that he had heard her sing and that she had invaded his thoughts long before they met.

"I just have to go inside for a couple of minutes to pick up my pay," Monique said, turning off the engine.

"I'll wait here," he said.

"You probably should. My boss would take one look at your swollen face and Charlie would probably be without a job," she said. "He works here too, you know."

The night air was relentlessly hot, and without the advantage of a breeze, the immobile car was instantly broiling. As

108

Adam reached down and opened the window, a pain shot through his shoulder, a recurring discomfort he still hadn't learned to anticipate. "Jesus," he mumbled as he reached up and rubbed it.

"Charlie's got arthritis," Monique offered as she got out of the car.

"Oh? Well at least he doesn't have my stomach problems," he said.

"Yeah, I guess everyone's got their crosses. Right?" she asked, as she pushed the heavy door shut.

A twinge of anger pecked at Adam, who again felt as if he were needlessly on trial. "Whatever," he grumbled as she walked into the dark bar.

From the car, Adam could see Monique approach the short, heavy Jimmy, who was seated on the stage which was raised a foot off the ground. He sat behind the piano, with a cigar hanging from his ample jowl, punching unenthusiastically on the ivory keys when he noticed Monique walking toward him.

"Moon!" he exclaimed, a smile stretching across his face as if she had awakened him from a bad dream. He immediately abandoned the piano in mid-song, leaving a skinny, sallow young singer without a note to accompany her. Her voice trailed off in an awkward tone, falling to a whisper, then to silence. She too looked at Monique and smiled.

"Hi, Moon," she said softly. Her manner was reserved and shy, quite the opposite of most entertainers in the Vieux Carre'.

"Hey Sara . . . Jimmy," Monique said. "Jimmy I need to talk to you."

Jimmy looked out into the sparse audience at an exceptionally bored looking group of Midwesterners clustered around a small table.

"Hey, this is my main singer," he called out proudly.

109

"Moon, this is my brother and his family all the way from Kansas."

Monique smiled politely in the direction of the family. "Nice to see you all." Then she turned back to Jimmy with business on her mind.

"Jimmy I'm here for my pay," she said quietly and somewhat urgently.

Turning a deaf ear to her request, he looked past her shoulder, out the door at Adam seated in the car.

"Hey, Charlie, come on in," he called out.

"No, Jimmy, we've got to go," she said, but before she could catch him, he was already out the door.

Adam saw the squatty man headed in his direction and tried to look the other way. Although Jimmy had repaid his loan in a timely manner, Adam had hated doing business with him. He was a pushy, spoiled little man who made his nerves dance with irritation. The last thing Adam wanted was to face him while trapped in the guise of a feeble, stammering kid who was at the disadvantage of being his employee. When Adam realized that, in spite of his attempt to ignore him, Jimmy was still headed toward the car, he reached down and started to roll up the window.

"Charlie, come on in," Jimmy said thrusting his hand inside the glass to stop Adam from closing it.

Adam, surrendering to the inevitable, turned toward him, and when he did, his bruised and bloody face was revealed in the street lights.

"Lord have mercy, what happened to you?" Jimmy gasped.

"Jimmy, leave him alone, he's not feeling good," Monique said nervously.

"Well, I can see why. Looks like you been hanging out with the wrong crowd Mr. Charles," he scolded. "I'm a sympathetic man, but you better heal up pretty quick," he warned. "I can't be going without a sax."

"He'll be fine, Jimmy. Now will you give me my pay so we can get outta here?" she asked.

Jimmy removed the cigar from his crinkled lips. "Okay, but first you gotta sing for my family."

"This isn't a good time, Jimmy," Monique said.

"Come on. You can't expect me to impress them with that spindly little chirper, can you?" he asked pointing to Sara who was standing awkwardly at the bar.

"I'm not in the mood to sing. Besides, there's nothing wrong with Sara," she replied.

"No sing, no pay," he argued stubbornly.

"Can't you see this is a really bad time?" she asked, but her argument wasn't good enough to please her obstinate boss. He stuck the cigar back in his mouth and pursed his lips around it in silence.

"Jimmy, you're a shithead, you know that? I don't even have a blouse," she countered angrily.

"What happened to your shirt?" the little man asked, pulling open her jacket to reveal her bra underneath. Monique slapped his hand back, as a whistle came from a couple of teenagers walking along the opposite side of the street.

"Hey you little mudbugs! Mind your own business," Jimmy yelled out at the admirers. "I'll get you a shirt," he said, encouraged at the prospect of a song.

"All right, Jimmy, one song," she said.

"Two," he quipped.

"One. And you're paying me overtime for this," she informed him.

"I'll be out in a second," she said to Adam before following her boss inside.

111

* * * * *

Jimmy headed behind the bar and pulled out an old work shirt.

"Oh great, Tex's smelly shirt," she said to Jimmy as she pulled off her jacket and put it on. "This ought to make a great impression." She tied the red plaid shirt in front, and in spite of her complaints, it was quite flattering to her fair complexion.

She hopped up onto the stage and grabbed the microphone with the ease she had shown for years. As she stood with the tiny lights shining in her eyes, she suddenly became aware of Adam watching her from the car and for the first time since she could remember, butterflies began battling it out in her stomach. She hoped that Jimmy would pick something quick and simple.

"You're going to love her," he called out to his family. "She usually packs the place."

"Jimmy," she hissed, signaling for him to shut up and play.

His fingers went slowly down on the keys, forming the melody to a mellow blues song. Upon hearing the tender notes, Monique's heart thumped heavily as she prepared to begin the song, but her nervousness caused her to lose her train of thought and Jimmy had to go through another round of chords to get back to the starting point. This is ridiculous, she thought, and forced herself to look into the lights that took the rest of the world away, replacing it with a warm, calm feeling. She closed her eyes and let her head fall back as she swayed with the melody.

Her voice sounded in a sad, rich tone, drifting through the smoky door of the bar, out onto the dark deserted street. Although Adam loved the sound of her voice, there was something about it that he found disconcerting. He lay his head back

112

on the seat, closed his eyes and tried to relax, but the more she sang, the more anxious he became. An aching pit began to pull at his insides, leaving him uneasy and off-balance. He tried to concentrate on something other than the melancholy song or the bizarre day. Business had always been his lifeline, only now it seemed so far away and unimportant. He thought about his wife and pondered what she could be doing at that moment. He tried to think back on what they had done Thursday night and he remembered that he had spent it working while his wife was out at a ladies' gathering. Although the thought of her didn't disturb him, it didn't comfort him, either. As it was, he had no urge to see her. His mind drifted to his son, Philip, but he instantly tried to change the subject because thoughts of the gaunt child only compounded the aching feeling. Although he loved his son deeply, he felt completely inadequate as a father. It seemed the harder he tried to give the boy direction, the skinnier the child became. Adam sighed heavily, rubbing the base of his neck. As he lay back, struggling with his thoughts, he suddenly became aware of someone breathing over him. He bolted from his slouched position and began wrestling with the intruder who was leaning in the car.

"Son-of-a-bitch," he said as he shoved the smelly body back out the window. An elderly man, dressed in the dark clothes of a bum, stumbled back from the car looking terrified.

"I . . . I just wanted a cigarette," he cried, trembling with fear, his glassy little eyes blinking with apology.

Adam saw on the dashboard what the old man had been after. A half-used pack of Marlboros lay in front of him, apparently too much for the old man to resist. He grabbed them from the dash and thrust them out to the tattered beggar.

"Here take 'em," he said.

"No, no, I just wanted one," the old man said as he gingerly

113

pulled one from the pack while it was still in Adam's hand. "I'm trying to quit," he said with a shaky smile, then clenched the cigarette between his brown teeth. He stood staring down at Adam as if waiting for something more. Finally, he put words to his request. "How about a light?"

Adam looked at him a moment, then decided the only way to get rid of him was to oblige him.

"I didn't mean to scare you," the bum apologized as Adam pulled a book of matches from the side of the pack, struck one and held it up to the old man's cigarette. He took a puff, then cocked his tiny head to the side. "That voice," he said in admiration of Monique's melody which floated through the air like an intoxicating perfume. "Such a lovely voice."

"Did you want these or not?" Adam asked impatiently.

"No, thank you son," he said, then, as if taking the hint, nodded his head, then continued down the street, his worn shoes scuffling along slowly.

Feeling jittery and restless, Adam tossed the cigarettes back onto the dash and got out of the car. He paced up and down the sidewalk, anything to escape the forlorn song and desolate surroundings. Not one to indulge his emotions, he felt deeply resentful of the bombarding discomfort they were creating. As he passed by the car, the pack of Marlboros shone through the front window at him. To his own surprise, he reached into the car and picked them up and even though he had never smoked before, he pulled one out and placed it between his lips.

"I don't believe this," he muttered to himself, as he struck a match and awkwardly lit it up. He took a long deep drag, half expecting to cough it back up, but instead found great relief in the soothing smoke. "The dumb shit smokes," he said aloud with repugnance.

He took another drag and continued to pace along the sidewalk. After a moment, he stopped and looked down at the burning cigarette, placed between two fingers of the rough hand. Staring down at the pathetic sight, he felt the avenging sadness return. "Why do all you poor bastards smoke?" he asked aloud, then quickly threw the cigarette to the cement and stamped it out with his shoe. Much to his relief, the song ended and an upbeat tune began, Jimmy apparently having gotten his way.

Adam peered into the doorway of the hazy bar, his eyes falling onto Monique illuminated in the stage lights. She was so vibrant and alive, putting everything she had into the jazzy song. Jimmy pounded away at the piano, sweat rolling off his fleshy face with a toothy smile spread wide. His family was tapping to the beat, their eyes glued to the gorgeous singer, whose enthusiasm and love for her work were contagious.

* * * * *

Jimmy rang open the register and pulled out Monique's pay in the form of cash.

"Here you go," he said sweetly handing the wad of bills to her.

"Thanks for cashing it for me, Jimmy," Monique smiled and then turned to leave.

"Wait, hang on," he called. "I found this on the floor the other night," he said holding up a chain with a locket on it.

Monique's face lit up upon seeing it. "I've been looking everywhere for that thing. Thanks. Maybe my luck will improve again," she said snatching it from his hand and heading out the door. "Tell Tex I'll give him his shirt back when he learns how to do his wash," she called back with a smile as she placed the necklace over her neck.

"Nice voice," Adam said after she passed through the door into the night air.

"Thanks," she said, thrown off guard by Adam's friendly compliment. "Sorry it took so long."

Chapter 14

Long shadows, created by a nearly full moon, streaked across the rear brick wall of the weathered apartment building. The clanking of Monique's feeble car bounced between the dense structures as she parked behind a motorcycle and shut off her headlights. The not so distant rumble of Bourbon Street could be heard, as she and Adam entered the back door thirty feet down from the fire exit he had stumbled out from that morning. Adam had not wanted to return to the building but he had no money and no where else to go. Besides, he was intent on making sure the loan got repaid so the nightmare could end.

Without the benefit of the morning sunlight, the inside of the apartment building appeared even danker at night than it had earlier that day. Bare light bulbs hung from the ceiling of the narrow hallway, the flooring and wallpaper had been unchanged for over twenty years. The building itself was part of the original rebuilding of the French Quarter after the great fire of Good Friday, 1788 and after many years of falling into disrepair, was preserved by the local Government of New Orleans along with the rest of the Vieux Carre'. It creaked and moaned with the many lives it had housed over the years, taking on a distinct personality of its own. In spite of the rich aroma of red beans and rice, frying oysters and other Cajun delights, the musty smell of the building was ever present.

Monique led the way down the thin corridor, but to Adam's confusion, stopped several doors short of her own apartment.

As she tapped lightly on the door, she noticed Adam's bewilderment.

"I need to get my baby," she explained.

The dark wooden door swung open revealing a tall, exceptionally thin black man, whom Adam recognized to be one of the musicians that backed Monique the first night he had heard her sing. It was the old man's name, which escaped Adam at the moment, that the barkers had flaunted so proudly in front of "Jimmy Blues" to lure the customers inside. They boasted that he was a well-known trumpet player who had formed the original "Daddy Pops" back in the sixties.

Upon seeing Monique, a bright smile spread across the old man's mischievous face. His kind eyes, which had seen many years of their own, were an amber brown accentuated by the myriad of deep wrinkles formed by seventy-two years of living. He wore a long sleeved cotton shirt with loose fitting trousers. The baggy pants, held up by suspenders, emphasized his towering height. A white cast covered his left forearm, his thin fingers with long nails hung out from it like a spider half inside a snow covered cave. With the exception of a few dark strands, his hair was mostly white. Even his eyebrows sprouted signs of his age.

"Well hello there, Moon," he said happily, but the smile quickly faded when he saw past her to Adam's bruised face.

"What happened to you?" he asked.

Adam was not sure how to respond to the kindly man and looked helplessly at Monique who nervously began stammering to explain as if she were a small child about to be scolded.

"Oh, he uh, got into a fight down at Jimmy's," she said with a beet red face, evidently unaccustomed to lying to the elderly man.

After thirty years of parenting Monique, the old man couldn't help but smile inside at how easily he could tell when the sweet child wasn't telling the truth. Monique cowered under his skeptical gaze.

"A fight?" he snapped.

"Yeah," she said for lack of better words.

He turned his knowing eyes to Adam. "That's not like you, Charlie," he said holding his gaze on him a moment. "Well, get your skinny little butt in here and let me fix you up," he commanded, disappearing through the doorway.

Adam looked to Monique for advice. He could tell she was uneasy by the way she squeezed her hands together. "Let's go in," she finally said.

"What's his name?" Adam asked before entering, thinking it a good thing to know in case he was forced into conversation with the old man.

"Wilton Young. He's my dad," she answered, much to his amazement. It seemed absurd that such a fair skinned woman could have a black man for a father. "Please," she continued anxiously, "I don't want to upset him! He's very old and—"

"Are you two gonna stand out there all night?" Wilton called from within.

*   *   *   *   *

The apartment was very cozy, containing all the clutter and knickknacks it takes a lifetime to accumulate. As Monique and

Adam entered the living room, the floor squeaked with varying rhythms and inflections as if speaking a language all its own. A large overstuffed burgundy couch dominated the room. The tiny Amy was snuggled within a colorful quilt, her curly blonde hair lying softly on a pillow, her pink lips curled up in sweet slumber.

"How's my little puddin'?" Monique cooed, brimming with love for the toddler. Unable to resist her daughter's rosy cheeks, Monique smooched her soft skin. She wanted so badly to wake her up and squeeze her tightly, but knowing the child needed all the rest she could get, she managed a little bit of self restraint.

Adam stood uncomfortably, feeling more like an intruder than ever. He glanced about the room at various childhood photos of Monique, amazed by the resemblance between her and the sleeping child. In one of the pictures, a very young Monique was seated at a piano on Jimmy's lap, with a middle-aged Wilton standing beside them. There were also many recent photos of Monique, Charlie and Amy, tucked in every available nook and cranny. Wilton's family was clearly the center of his life. He joined them in some of the photos, forming an unconventional family. They all seemed so happy together and closer than most families, certainly closer than Adam's.

"She had a rough day," Wilton said, pulling something from the belly of a large antique china cabinet that stood like a gorilla holding its ground in the corner of the room. "I didn't have the heart to move her to the bedroom."

Adam awkwardly took a seat, failing desperately to appear casual. Although he found Wilton to be a pleasant man and didn't want to cause any trouble for Monique by further invading her privacy, he was truly tired of the whole charade of not knowing what to say or do. He leaned his head against his hand and sat in silence.

"Here you go," Wilton said, holding out a wad of cash to Monique.

When Monique saw the money a sigh of relief came across her face and she looked over at Adam as if to say everything was going to be okay. "Oh Wilton, you're an angel," she said, taking the money and leaping to her feet to kiss him on his whiskery cheek.

"Don't start with the mush," he said with unconvincing resistance and put his arms up to protest her kisses, even though he clearly enjoyed the affection.

Monique stuffed the money into her pocket. "We'll pay you back, I promise."

"Nonsense," he argued. "You should have asked me for the money in the first place, instead of borrowing from a stranger."

Monique's face again went crimson because she hadn't told Wilton the complete truth about where the loan had originated. "The money came from a friend of Jimmy's," she had said, leaving out that "friend" was the operative word.

"I don't care what you say, we're paying you back," she insisted, her full lips clenching tight.

Wilton threw Adam a devious grin. "She was born pigheaded and stayed that way." Uncomfortable with the undeserved comradery, Adam remained silent. Wilton noticed Adam's discomfort and focused his wise old eyes upon him, studying him closely. Adam squirmed in his seat, as the humor fell from the old man's face, and was replaced with an expression of graveness. "Take him in the kitchen and clean him up, while I get my medicine box," he instructed Monique.

Copper pots and cast iron pans hung over the gas stove, the wallpaper behind them dulled to light brown from many years of melting steam and frying food. The kitchen was small with a tiny table supported by steel legs and covered with a checkered table-cloth made of plastic. Although it was a modest kitchen, it was very clean in every way. The window, which faced the back alley, was propped open with a wooden stick. Potted flowers were perched on the window sill, their sweet fragrance drifting in with the warm, sultry air.

Monique removed a bowl from the cabinet and began filling it with warm water. "Have a seat," she said, motioning Adam to the table. He obediently sat down on the vinyl covered chair, and scooted it up to the table, while Monique brought the bowl of water and a towel to his side. She inspected the blood which had dried like paste onto his skin, then dipped the cloth into the steaming water, wrung it out and touched it to his brow. He immediately pulled back.

"Sorry," she said, then leaned closer to him and wiped his brow again more gently. Adam could feel her soft breath on his cheek as she dabbed at the cut.

"Is he really your father?" he asked quietly.

"He raised me," she said as she dipped the cloth back into the water, staining the liquid pinkish red.

"What happened to your parents?" he questioned.

Monique paused, as if hesitant to answer. "Believe it or not, I was born into a wealthy family in Mobile," she finally said. "My mother died when I was three and my father, who never wanted children in the first place, just sort of forgot that I was there."

"So how did you end up with Wilton?" he asked.

"He worked as our gardener, and after my mom died, he took me under his wing," she said. Adam could see the deep admiration she held for the old man. He watched her closely as the warmth left her face and her eyes became vacant.

122

"Then, out of the blue, my father packed me up and took me to an adoption agency," she said quietly, looking intently into the bowl of blood as she wrung out the rag. "The next day, Wilton came and got me and moved me here."

"Hmm," Adam said.

"What?" she asked, looking up at him.

"Oh I don't know. It just seems strange that they would let a middle-aged black man adopt you," he said.

"Oh, are you kidding?" she laughed. "That would have been too scandalous for my father's political career. No, Wilton just convinced him that putting me up for adoption would be an occupational hazard, regardless of who adopted me. So it was agreed that Wilton could raise me but only if he left the state."

"Your father is a politician?" he asked.

"Yes."

"Who is he?" he asked, but judging by the look on Monique's face, he knew his question would go unanswered.

After a moment of silence a tender smile came across her face. Although there was a distraction about her, she seemed more relaxed than Adam had ever seen her and the result was quite lovely. "I couldn't have asked for a better dad than Wilton," she said with contentment, then returned once again to cleansing his face.

"That child might just sleep all night," Wilton said as he entered carrying a leather bag.

"Let me see," he said, taking Adam by the chin and holding his face up to the light that hung overhead. "Looks like your eye got the worst of it," he said pulling open the bag to reveal all sorts of medical paraphernalia. "You can do without stitches, but I better bandage it up for a couple of days." He pulled out a Tylenol bottle filled with a homemade salve and applied it to

Adam's brow. Adam could smell the strange mixture, and wondered what in the world it could be. As if reading his mind, Monique smiled.

"That's Wilton's special miracle goo," she said chuckling at Adam's squeamishness. "Isn't that right, Pop?"

"MMhhhmmm," he mumbled, concentrating on the cut. As he took a cotton bandage from the bag and leaned over Adam to apply it, the sleeve on his right arm fell back, revealing a large gash to his own flesh. "You need to be more careful," he reprimanded Adam.

"Looks like I'm not the only one," Adam replied, noticing the hideous injury.

Monique looked up to see what Adam was referring to, just as Wilton quickly pulled his sleeve back down.

"Let me see that!" she exclaimed, moving toward Wilton.

"Get back, I'm fine," Wilton said. "I just fell down those damn front steps."

"Again?" she asked.

Wilton went back to doctoring Adam. "Now hush, or you'll have me thinking I'm too old to look after Amy." Then, as if suddenly realizing that Adam had spoken without a stutter, Wilton's mouth dropped open. "Charlie? Did I hear you right?"

Monique, who was at the sink rinsing out the bloody bowl, stiffened, then looked nervously back at Adam. Unsure how to answer, Adam reached his hand to his jaw.

"I guess maybe they knocked something into place," he said quietly.

Wilton's face became radiant with happiness. "Well, I'll be!" he exclaimed. "You're like a new person," he said shaking his head in disbelief. "I've never heard of such a thing. Hell, if I'd known that would cure you, I would have slapped you around myself," he said with a grin.

"Well, don't get too used to it, because stutters come back sometimes," Monique said, looking in Adam's direction. "In fact, I prefer it," she said coolly.

Wilton rummaged through the medical bag looking for a roll of tape. While shuffling the contents about, various syringes and insulin fell out onto the table. Adam saw the paraphernalia and remembered that Monique had said her child was sick.

"Are those for Amy?" he asked.

Wilton was astounded by the question. "Amy? Good Lord, no! Why would a child with asthma take insulin?"

"Wilton's diabetic," Monique quickly offered.

"Charlie, you know that. Looks like that stutter's not all they knocked lose," he countered.

Monique cringed at the thought of the fierce blows she had been forced to witness. Suddenly, she remembered that Kyle and Marshal were supposed to be coming by at 9:30 to pick up the money she had promised. Trepidation came over her as she looked to the broken kitchen clock which perpetually read 11:55. It must be at least 9:30, she thought, quickly going to the window. Much to her dread, she found Kyle's Cadillac parked in the alley below. She squinted to see if they were in the car but she couldn't tell from her angle. The thought of them on their way up to her apartment made her heart skip a beat. She looked anxiously over at Wilton who seemed to be working at a snail's pace in finishing up the first aid job. "Uh, Charlie, I'd really like to be getting home," she blurted.

Wilton pushed down the last piece of tape. "Well, go on then," he prodded. He noticed Monique's strange hesitation. "He's a big boy. He can find his own way home."

With great reluctance, Monique backed a few steps in the

direction of the door. "Okay," she uttered. Once out of Wilton's sight, she broke into a run through the rest of the apartment toward the front door.

* * * * *

"Done," Wilton said and started putting the first aid items back into his bag.

Adam got up from the table and went to the window to see what had upset Monique. Kyle, now standing by his car, smiled and waved at him from below. Adam mused that if one didn't know better, they would think his brother was a friendly guy coming for a visit. Far be it from the truth.

"Thanks a lot," Adam said abruptly to the old man, then headed brusquely for the front door. Just as his hand touched the handle, he heard Wilton calling.

"Charlie? . . . Charlie?"

When he turned around, Wilton was standing in the living room with the sleeping Amy in his frail arms. "Ain't you forgettin' somethin'?" Wilton asked, puzzled by the new Charlie.

Adam stood still by the door, slightly bewildered by the situation. The last time he had held the little toddler, she had been cold with death. He remembered her tiny body falling into the dark hole he had dug, and the mounds of dirt he had piled upon her. It now seemed terribly wrong for him to take the innocent child into his care.

"Well?" Wilton urged.

Adam, seeing no other choice, slowly walked toward Wilton to retrieve the child. As he drew closer, he noticed that Wilton's big amber eyes were filled with glassy tears. Startled by the

126

sight, Adam didn't know what to do or say. Wilton looked lovingly down at the sleeping toddler. "Take good care of my baby. She's the closest thing to a grandchild I got," he said, the tears running down his cheeks. With shaky arms, he bent to kiss Amy on the forehead, then held her out for Adam to take. Adam reluctantly stepped forward and took the child. She snuggled up into his arms, the warmth of her tiny body next to his chest.

"And watch over my Moon, too," Wilton continued. "Never let her forget that I loved her with all my heart."

Adam was slightly confused by the elderly man's display of emotions. Although he had walked into a very personal moment without the slightest clue as to what was going on, he was none the less touched by it. Wilton's sad face stared at him imploringly.

"You'll do that for me, won't you son?"

Adam, feeling like a traitor, was at a complete loss for words. If only the old man knew what he was asking. He was entrusting the most precious gifts he had ever received to the very person who had caused their deaths. "Sure," Adam heard himself say.

A beaming smile spread across Wilton's face. "I knew I could count on you. You're a good man."

* * * * *

Inside Monique's apartment, she pulled apart the couch, cushion by cushion, frantically searching for the envelope of money she had placed there only a few days earlier. "Come on, come on," she whispered, fearing she wouldn't find the money and really wouldn't be able to pay back the loan. Just as she was losing hope, her hand came across the crispy paper, wedged low in the couch, apparently having worked its way down by normal use of the sofa. She pulled it out, counted the money, then placed the bills that Wilton had given her alongside the rest.

She turned anxiously for the door and was surprised to find Adam standing in front of her holding Amy in his arms. Off centered with the situation, they both looked at one another in silence.

"She's a beautiful child," Adam said in a whisper, then gently handed her to Monique.

"Yes she is," she smiled faintly. As she remembered the envelope still in her hand, a cold chill replaced the tender moment. She handed the money to Adam. "Your thugs are out back," she said, her voice devoid of all warmth. "Why don't you keep the appointment?"

Adam silently took the envelope and started down the hallway. He knew the couple owed him the money, yet he felt awful being the one to deliver it. In spite of the slight pang of guilt, he took comfort in the fact that the loan was being repaid, therefore no one would be hurt.

Monique watched him as he disappeared down the stairs, then slowly and gently closed the door.

* * * * *

The intense moonlight made Kyle's face seem longer and more pallid than usual. He leaned against the car, Marshal seated inside with his cheek mashed against the passenger window in a deep sleep.

As Adam approached, he noticed a middle-aged woman,

128

who happened to be passing by with her groceries, stop and take note of Kyle. Upon drawing closer, Adam saw that Kyle had a vial stuck to his nose. In disbelief of his brother's blatant disregard for the law, anger shot through his veins. "I can't believe you're doing that right out in public," he exclaimed before he could catch himself. Kyle looked up at him a little amazed. He turned to the gawking woman, and shooed her on with a nasty smirk.

"You're not exactly in a position to be giving advice, stick man," Kyle retorted, holding the empty vial up to the street lamp to check if he got all the powder. "Marshal, fill this back up," he ordered, tossing the empty container onto the front seat. "I believe in recycling," he announced with a smile. "It's my contribution to Planet Earth. Do you have my money?"

Adam saw Monique look through the curtains of her apartment above as he handed Kyle the envelope. After he had given it to him, she disappeared back through the parted curtains.

"Five thousand on the nose," Kyle said, counting the last of the stack of bills. As he placed the money into his wallet, Adam noticed Kyle's diamond pinkie ring. It had never bothered him before, but for some reason it now appeared so sleazy, filling him with a strange feeling of distrust.

"We'll be back in a week for the interest," Kyle said, opening his car door, the interior light spilling out into the alley.

Adam wasn't sure he had heard correctly. "Wait a minute, that's already included. That's all they owe."

Kyle gave him an odd, friendly look as he shut his car door. "I'll check the books," he promised, then started his engine.

The remark didn't rest well with Adam. He watched the car turn out of the alley, weighing the words in his mind. He considered the possibility of an accounting error, but then quickly discarded the worry by reassuring himself that Kyle had always run the business well. With new-found relief, he turned for the door. As he approached the darkened archway, a tall man stepped out of the shadows. It was Wilton.

"Them men gave you that beatin', didn't they?" he asked, his voice sounding much older than before.

Adam stood motionless, once again at a loss for words.

"No need to answer," Wilton said wearily. "Moon thinks I don't know you two borrowed that money from a shark," he said and then chuckled to himself. "That's okay. I won't tell her I know. But I got to ask you to keep a secret for me, too, Charlie."

Here we go, Adam thought. He was eager to get back to being Adam Claiborne again and to return these people to their own lives and secrets. He hated the trust the old man kept bestowing upon him. He put his hand up to smooth his hair, but it didn't have the usual calming affect it normally did just by virtue of the fact that it wasn't his hair.

"Listen, uh—" he said.

"Please," Wilton interrupted. "I just want you to keep her away from those kind of people. They're no good. I know it's hard to tell Monique what to do, she'll just go off and do it anyway. All I want is for you to keep an eye on her. That's all . . . and not tell her I know about your trouble with these guys," he said gravely. "That Kyle is very troubled . . . very troubled."

Adam wondered how Wilton knew Kyle's name if Monique or Charlie hadn't told him.

"Just do as I ask, okay?" Wilton asked.

"Sure," Adam said awkwardly.

Chapter 15

Adam creaked open the front door, unsure whether or not to knock before entering the apartment. Monique, having changed into a red flowered robe, clenched a lumpy down pillow under her chin, tugging with a faded pillow case.

"You can come in," she said, successfully wrangling the pillow into its cover. She dropped it onto the swayed couch beside a set of sheets. "We're not used to overnight guests from the Garden District, so you'll have to pardon our old bed clothes."

In spite of the meager furnishings of the room, it was a pleasantly colorful living room. Decorative rugs hung from the walls, candles and family photos splashed everywhere. Although the hardwood floors were scratched, the protective varnish worn off by many years of use, the golden wood added a charm that carpeting often muffled. Through a curtain of bright beads, which divided the kitchen from the living room, Adam could see a pot boiling on the ancient gas stove.

"That's red beans and rice if you're hungry," she said noticing his glance to the kitchen.

"No, thanks, I'm really not," he said.

The apartment, having been closed up all day, was exceptionally hot, and although Monique had propped open a window with a stick, it was still steaming. A set of chimes hung limp above the window sill, only occasionally played by the faint breeze which carried no relief from the heat. Adam wiped the sweat from his brow and looked about the room for an air conditioner. He didn't see one and doubted they could afford the luxury of central air.

"I gave him the money, so everything should be okay," he said as if to reassure her. She turned her beautiful face toward him, her cheek bones accentuated by the angle of the warm light illuminating from a lamp on the end table. She was a sturdy woman and yet so feminine. "Good," she said simply, a whisper of perspiration glistening above her lips.

He found it difficult to meet her gaze for long, her beauty stirring within him an attraction he couldn't deny. As he looked away from her sumptuous lips, his eyes were caught by her necklace. Although she had been wearing it ever since she left Jimmy Blues, it was the first time that he noticed it. The charm that dangled from the delicate chain was unmistakably the same one that he had found on the ground after killing her and Charlie. She noticed him looking strangely down at it and brought her hand to touch it. "What is it?" she asked.

He remembered how frightened Kyle had been of the trinket. "I recognize that necklace," he said, the words seeming to stick in his throat.

"It's for good luck," she said.

"Your husband was wearing it along with a St. Christopher's medal."

"Well, it wasn't my husband's then. He doesn't have a St. Christopher's medal and I'm the only one who ever wears this. It must have been someone else's," she concluded.

"No, it was his," he said, remembering how it had fallen from Charlie's dead body outside of the cellar. "Kyle was terrified by it. He said it was voodoo."

"Well, your brother, Kyle, obviously doesn't understand

132

voodoo if he was scared of this," she said.

Adam began to feel uneasy, wondering if maybe he had un-
derestimated the power of the charm. "You and your husband
practice voodoo?"

Upon hearing the tone in Adam's voice, Monique smiled at
the irony of the situation. Although she was no stranger to defending her practice against outside scrutiny, she felt somewhat
indignant in having to justify her beliefs to a man who committed
murder then expected his faith to condone it. But so many people
had misunderstood her religion and judged her based on what
they thought they knew of it. Although she had been born into a
Catholic family, that was not the religion Wilton had raised her
by after he brought her to New Orleans. He had tried for several
years to keep up her family's religious beliefs but had a hard time
teaching something he didn't completely understand himself.
Finally, he had to turn back to his own faith of voodooism in order to successfully instill the morals and spirituality she needed.
Although he knew that she would face ridicule, especially since it
was predominantly a black man's religion, he knew no other way.
He decided the only way for her to overcome the criticism was to
educate her about where the ridicule, which was largely based on
fear, came from. He began by teaching her the history of voodoo,
explaining that it originated in Africa, and it wasn't until slavery
that it made its way to the United States. The slaves continued to
practice their colorful rituals much to the consternation of the
Christian plantation owners, who found voodoo to be savagely
foreign. The practice was soon outlawed and forced under-
ground, and like anything that becomes taboo it eventually turned
to the occult. As the slaves stole away into the night, a dark mys-
tique began to surround the forbidden practices. Black magic,
which was a mutant form of voodoo, began to feed the wagging
tongues of the Bible wielding Christians. Little did they know it

was their own teachings that added the dark element to the strictly positive beliefs of the Africans, who had never even heard of the devil until they were exposed to the Christian missionaries of Haiti.

Wilton had cautioned Monique many times to avoid black magic, teaching her that the true form of voodoo never intended evil. Wilton believed in a loving, gentle God and it was for this reason he felt it was a good stronghold for Monique who had become his sole responsibility. She had been raised in a positive, loving environment, without the grim tales of a vengeful God and the looming perils of Hell.

In order to fill the gap between Monique and her peers, Wilton had pointed out the similarities of voodoo to other, more mainstream religious beliefs. He explained how the slaves adapted to their new world by integrating voodoo with Catholicism after they realized the two religions were not so dissimilar after all. As it was though, when Monique had argued this point to many appalled Catholics, she usually ended up alienating herself from them. Although Wilton did the best he could in raising her, he often regretted the pain she had been exposed to in trying to assimilate two such different cultures. He felt that if her skin were less alabaster and her hair darker, she would have adjusted with much more ease to his world.

Monique knew too well the judgmental, frightened eyes that stared back at her, and considering that the fear was coming from Adam Claiborne, she felt a twinge of anger.

"You know what really amazes me? You see yourself as the victim here," she said, her face flushed by his arrogant scrutiny of her beliefs. "Charlie didn't put some kind of hex on you if that's what you're thinking."

"But you do practice voodoo?" Adam demanded, growing more and more convinced of its power and its possible implications to his freakish situation.

The hint of a smile twitched at the corners of Monique's mouth. For once she would derive pleasure from the all too familiar argument.

"Yes we practice voodoo, but before you start judging me, I think you ought to know that we've got more in common than you may think. Voodoo practices are not that far away from Catholicism," she quipped.

"What are you talking about?" Adam retorted, offended at once by the ludicrous accusation.

"You see that cross up there?" she asked, pointing to a brass ornament hung over the front doorway. "That's the Cross of Carvaca to pray to St. Benito. We say Hail Marys, and Our Fathers and all sorts of Catholic prayers. Correct me if I'm wrong but you pray to saints, don't you?"

Adam was silent, deeply resenting the bizarre piece of information.

"You use candles to burn beneath their statues as offerings. We do the same only our candles are different colors that represent different needs," she said. "And none of those needs are to inflict harm."

"Then why do you stuff a dead claw into a locket like some kind of curse," he countered.

Monique looked down for a moment to try and regain her composure, then looked back up at him with decisiveness.

"Did you have a rabbit's foot when you were a child?" she asked.

Adam was thrown by the strange question. "What do you mean?" he asked.

"A rabbit's foot. A dead one. Did you have one?" she repeated.

The direct comparison between the dead claw and the dead

foot hit Adam. He stood dumbfounded by the unexpected turn of the conversation. "Yes," he answered with reluctance, feeling like a mouse within the razor sharp fangs of a tomcat.

"Your rabbit's foot isn't any different from this alligator's claw," she countered, opening the locket, exposing the nutria inside. "People carry them for the same reasons. A rabbit's foot brings you good luck because it makes you cautious and quick, like a rabbit. It endows you with the qualities of the animal. An alligator's claw brings you good luck because they're patient and quick," she concluded, snapping the locket shut between her tense fingers. "Please, tell me the difference."

Adam stared down at the tiny trinket in bewilderment, feeling a little foolish.

"This necklace didn't put you where you are right now, no more than a rabbit's foot or a St. Christopher's medal," she argued.

He slowly met her flashing eyes.

"Me and Charlie are the victims here, not you. We didn't do this to you. You did it to yourself," she concluded, then turned abruptly toward her bedroom.

Chapter 16

Marshal found it somewhat difficult to keep up with his boss's lilting gait as they made their way through the French Quarter toward the Royal Cafe located on the corner of Bourbon and Iberville. Kyle was in particularly high spirits after receiving the payment of five thousand from the Sinclairs. Even though they were scheduled to meet Adam Claiborne at the restaurant thirty minutes ago, he had insisted on making a pit stop to his dealer first to renew his supply of "pleasure", as he so discreetly termed it. As Marshal struggled to keep pace, rivers of sweat were flowing from the fleshy rolls of fat around his neck. He tended to perspire in excess whenever on edge . . . and the anticipation of Claiborne's reprimands for their repeated tardiness was more than his glands could handle.

As Kyle and Marshal turned to enter the upscale restaurant, the barkers along Bourbon fought to lure them into the seedier establishments. Although the two gentlemen were dressed with a certain amount of wealth, their taste in clothing reflected their lack of class. This fact was not lost on the barkers who argued they'd be happier watching a nude dancer than sucking on a pricey bottle of wine. The rustlers would have won the battle if it hadn't been for Kyle and Marshal's prior commitment with the older Claiborne.

Marshal, whose nostrils flared at the enticing aroma of barbecued shrimp and blackened catfish, followed awkwardly behind Kyle as he indiscreetly bypassed the host of the posh restaurant, into the main dining area. They immediately spotted Claiborne seated at a table in the corner of the candle-lit room, a half empty cup of coffee in front of him.

"Now you've done it," Marshal hissed angrily into Kyle's ear. "He's probably been here forever."

Kyle shot him a glance, then slid into the booth next to his brother, dropping a red plastic money pouch onto the table beside the coffee cup.

"You're late," Claiborne grumbled, the sheen of his dark hair accenting his strong jaw line.

Kyle ignored the comment and casually glanced about the dining room, as Marshal nervously watched Claiborne open the pouch and count the money inside.

"Yeah, we had some problems," Marshal said, compensating for Kyle's lack of interest.

Claiborne finished counting the money, placed it back in the pouch then looked up at his two employees. It annoyed him that Kyle had fixed his greedy eyes upon a young teenage girl seated at the next table with her family.

"This is it?" Claiborne asked pointedly. "Three thousand dollars?"

"There was a couple of cops following us around all night," Kyle said, his gaze remaining on the girl.

"Yeah, it made it extra hard to get things done," Marshal quickly added.

"Cops?" Claiborne asked.

"Yeah," Marshal offered, "undercover cops."

Claiborne sat for a moment pondering the dilemma. He had never had to deal with the police before except the time Kyle ran into a drug problem.

"What are they following you around for?" he asked his brother, turning a scrupulous eye upon him. "Are you in trouble again?"

Kyle sat up a little straighter. "Why do you always assume it's something I've done?" he asked in defense.

"Because it usually is something you've done," Claiborne retorted.

"Having me bail out Sinclair wasn't exactly a smart idea," Kyle argued. "That's probably what got them on our tails."

Claiborne sat for a moment in consideration of his brother's point. "He doesn't do me any good in jail," he finally concluded.

"He doesn't do you any good out either," Kyle retorted, glad to put the blame elsewhere. "He only paid a thousand."

Claiborne looked up upon hearing the low amount. "She said she'd have all the money tonight," he said.

Kyle pulled a ledger from his pocket and leafed through it. "Yep. A thousand was it," he confirmed, shooting Marshal a silent but deadly threat against disputing his false claim.

Claiborne was clearly unhappy to hear the information. He felt a jab of anger at Monique for not keeping her promise. He thought for a long moment as the three men sat in silence. Kyle returned his gaze to the girl who smiled back at him. Her father noticed the exchange and glared over at him, but Kyle merely met his protective leer with a lusty grin and a lick of his lips.

"If they can't pay, they can earn it," Claiborne finally said, breaking the silence that had drenched Marshal's neck in a new batch of perspiration. "We'll have them do your rounds for a couple of weeks, until the cops get off our butts."

Marshal began choking on his own saliva. Kyle looked angrily over at him. "Just a cough," Marshal managed to say, trying to clear his throat. Even though he was still a very strong stout man, his age had left him more squeamish than he had ever imagined becoming. He didn't know the depth of Claiborne's anger and didn't want to find out. Even Kyle, who had been so nonchalant, seemed a little rattled by Claiborne's idea.

"I don't think that's such a good plan," Kyle said, deciding he'd better pay closer attention before things got out of hand.

"Why not?" his brother demanded.

Kyle and Marshal both sat helplessly silent, neither one able to come up with a plausible excuse why the Sinclairs couldn't do the rounds. Claiborne took their silence as nothing more than incompetence. "You follow behind at a safe distance to make sure they get the hang of it," he instructed.

Suddenly, a devious smile filled Kyle's face. "Maybe you should come along," he proposed, much to Marshal's astonishment. "That way you can see for yourself that the rounds get made."

Marshal went pale at the absurd suggestion and looked at Kyle as if he had lost his mind. He worked his foot over to Kyle's leg and nudged him forcefully with his toe. Kyle swiftly ground the heel of his boot onto Marshal's toes, which were insufficiently protected by his Italian loafers.

Claiborne, unaware of the war waging beneath the table, threw a five-dollar bill beside his coffee cup and stood up.

"Pick me up in the morning, but use Marshal's car instead of yours. The cops shouldn't be looking for his," he ordered.

Just then, the middle-aged maitre'd, dressed in a tux, approached the table. "Excuse me, sir," he interrupted, directing his words to Kyle. "I'm sorry, but I must request that you not harass the other customers. It seems the gentleman seated across from you found it necessary to remove his daughter from your presence."

Kyle could feel his brother's disapproving eyes upon him as

140

he looked over to the empty table where the girl and her family had been seated. "Well you should have told the old geezer that his daughter has a mind of her own," he said on his own behalf.

"But sir, she couldn't have been a day over fourteen," the man argued.

"Hey, if there's grass on the field, 'play ball'," Kyle said, trying to make light of the situation. He looked to his brother with a smile, expecting him to join in on the joke, only to be met with a cold, angry stare.

The maitre'd was stunned by his lewd remark and stood speechless before him. Claiborne's face turned red with embarrassment at his brother's insolence. "I'm sorry for his conduct. We were just leaving," he replied coolly.

"That would be wise," he advised politely then turned to leave.

Kyle shrank under the fury of his brother's eyes. "Do you always have to humiliate me in public like this?" Claiborne asked, embittered with sadness for his brother's disgusting behavior. Without waiting for a reply, he abruptly turned and left the restaurant.

After Claiborne was out of earshot, Marshal looked angrily over at Kyle who was clearly shaken by his brother's disappointment in him. "Have you pickled your brain?" he whispered with vehemence.

Kyle looked distractedly over at Marshal. "What?"

"Asking him to make the rounds with us," Marshal demanded.

Remembering the pressing situation, Kyle turned his thoughts back to the task at hand. "Don't you have any sense?" he asked, snapping back into gear. "He'll see the rounds getting made. Right?"

"What rounds?" Marshal asked as if talking with a lunatic.

141

Kyle smiled at Marshal's lack of understanding. "You have no faith in the higher, more intelligent species such as myself. Think about it. We send them on the collection rounds, us following behind watching them at a safe distance. Now when it comes time to fork over the payments, and they're not there, who's my brother going to trust? He may not always show it but he's crazy about me, and you're his long time employee. He's not going to take the word of some sleazy couple from the French Quarter over ours."

A ray of understanding flickered in Marshal's puffy, tired eyes. He regretted getting mixed up with the Claiborne brothers.

"That's more like it," Kyle smiled.

Chapter 17

"You shouldn't have hesitated! When I send you out to follow someone, you do it," the booming voice of Sergeant Hadley bellowed, with flushed cheeks and bulging eyes. Detectives Briggs and Hays stood before him feeling like fools. Kyle had outsmarted them in the worst of ways. Losing someone after only a few short hours was the most embarrassing of foul ups for experienced detectives such as themselves. The sergeant paced back and forth in front of them as if his footsteps would stomp the orders into their brains. "I want you to find the Cadillac and don't let it out of your sight until I say otherwise. I don't care what you have to do, just stay on his butt," he growled. Briggs and Hays had both experienced their commander's anger. They knew that if they screwed up the assignment again they could end up directing traffic in some rundown part of the city where traffic cops are considered human targets by unappreciative motorists.

"Gotcha," Briggs said with fervor, then instantly regretted it, thinking it sounded sarcastic.

The sergeant looked at him as if he found him to be the most pathetic of creatures. "You'd better," he warned.

Chapter 18

Adam fully expected to wake up in his own bed after going to sleep that night, but after a few fitful hours of nightmares he awoke sweating profusely on the rickety old couch of Monique's. He wasn't sure what had drawn him from the hellish dreams his mind had submerged him into, but upon seeing the cracked ceiling overhead, he was instantly filled with apprehension. He worried that his plan to set things straight by delivering the money himself to Kyle wouldn't do the trick of restoring sanity back to his upside down world. He tried to reassure himself that everything would have to return to normal now that the loan was repaid. There would be no reason to kill the couple, therefore no reason to continue in Sinclair's body. Maybe he would just have to wait until the morning to enter his own body again.

As he tossed the situation around in his mind, he suddenly became aware of a gasping sound coming from Amy's bedroom. Monique's door flew open and she raced through the dark living room toward her child's room. Adam leapt from the sofa to help, but by the time he got to the doorway, Monique already had the toddler in her lap, with a canister of Proventil to the child's mouth.

Amy immediately stopped gasping and began crying softly. Monique lay the canister on the bed while continuing to hold the

144

shaking child. Monique's face was stricken with pain as she rocked the baby back and forth in her arms soothing her with her melodious voice.

"There, there," she whispered.

Amy's rapid breathing calmed significantly, her long lashes swaying closer and closer back to sleep.

Adam was mesmerized by the sight, his own nerves calmed by the gentle voice. "Is she all right?" he whispered.

Startled by his presence, Monique looked up to see him standing in the doorway.

"She's fine," she said, a weary look of relief in her own eyes.

Adam left the mother and child and went back to the living room which seemed lighter now that his eyes had adjusted to the moonlight streaming through the windows. A heavy foreboding pressed down upon him. What if something had gone wrong with the money? Maybe Kyle had lied to him about the amount the couple paid. He quickly discarded the thought from his mind, telling himself that Kyle did a lot of things that he disapproved of but he would never steal from him. Surely he would be back in his own body by morning. He sank down on the couch, hoping he had successfully altered the terrible chain of events the following day would bring.

Chapter 19

Briggs sat staring down at his bare arm, wondering what time it was. He figured it was probably around nine o'clock since the sun had been up for awhile, but he hated to guess. He thought of waking Hays to find out, but then quickly dismissed the idea. "At least it's Friday," he mumbled to himself, trying to look at the positive side of things. Waiting was a painful job for Briggs and it seemed as though they had been parked on the street outside Kyle's building for days. He and Hays had left the police station the previous night and headed straight to Kyle's address to wait for the Cadillac to return. They had waited for hours, until finally, around four in the morning, the car pulled into the drive of the old shabby duplex and Kyle staggered to his door. No one had left or entered the duplex since.

Briggs looked toward the old white building and wondered why a man of Kyle's supposed income would live in such a dump. The entire neighborhood was rundown beyond rejuvenation. He shook his head at the sight of the paint chipping away from the window sill. "Unbelievable," he muttered. He strained to see if there was any movement inside the apartment, but the reflection of the morning sun glared off the window. He figured it was pointless, anyway, to search for signs of life considering Kyle had practically crawled to his door in a stupor only a few hours earlier, and probably hadn't risen from bed yet.

Although Briggs was looking straight up at the bathroom window, he was unaware that Kyle was staring back out at him. Kyle had slept less than four hours and was irritated beyond belief at the annoying spectacle of the undercover car parked down his street. He sighed heavily then went over to the sink with a dirty razor in his hand. He swished it through the scummy water, plugged in the basin, then raised it to his half-shaven face. He had decided to be well groomed and on his best behavior to hopefully win back his brother's confidence. He heard a honk from the alley and turned in disgust. "Marshal you dumb ass," he muttered aloud.

* * * * *

Marshal's car was parked out back behind the apartment building with Marshal at the wheel and Claiborne in the front passenger seat. Marshal immediately regretted honking the horn when Claiborne shot him a disgusted look.

"Don't honk," Claiborne said, amazed at the man's stupidity.

Marshal's sweat glands set into action, getting an early start on the stressful day. "Sorry," he said meekly. He hated being alone with Claiborne and was relieved to see Kyle exit the back door and start down the stairway.

* * * * *

Adam opened his crusted-over eyes to decipher the strange sucking sound that had pulled him from a deep sleep. The morning sun assaulted his vision as he strained to see a man standing over him.

"Unlucky night, buddy?" he recognized Kyle's voice to ask. His sight cleared just as Kyle put the coke vial once again to his nose and snorted the remaining powder.

"Better than coffee to get a man jump-started in the morning," his brother said.

Morning! Adam leapt to his feet, horrified to find himself still in Monique's apartment. He looked down at the feeble body he continued to occupy and wondered what had gone wrong. He turned to Kyle who stood watching his strange behavior with amusement. Suddenly, he heard Monique scream from her bedroom, followed by the sound of a struggle. He shoved Kyle aside and bolted toward her aid.

Inside the warmly lit room, Monique was on one side of the bed with a large shotgun pointed at Marshal who stood on the other. Having been rudely awakened by the intruders, she appeared to be slightly disoriented. Her hair was tousled and her nightgown was twisted around her body as if she had been scuffling with Marshal and had managed to overpower him.

"Put your hands up," she commanded with the gun nestled against her bare shoulder.

Kyle poked his head in the door as Marshal obeyed her order. He let out a squeal of laughter at the sight of Marshal under siege by the woman. "You poor bastard," he roared. "Do you have this effect on all the women?"

The gun pivoted in his direction. "You too!" she ordered.

Although Monique was a strong woman with the shotgun tight within her grasp, Kyle didn't take the sight seriously. "Look, little lady, we're just . . . " he said, moving toward her, but then stopped suddenly when she forcefully cocked the gun with expertise.

148

"Do it," she said, clearly at ease with the large shotgun and fully prepared to use it.

"Yes, ma'am," Kyle conceded.

Monique looked uneasily over at Adam, unsure which side of the fence he would play. Adam met her eyes and saw the uncertainty. He knew that as long as he was in Charlie's body he would have to defend himself against his brother's violence. He made a move toward Kyle, who responded by pulling back from his advance.

"Don't move and my wife won't shoot," Adam warned, reaching behind Kyle's back and lifting his jacket. He removed the gun Kyle had tucked in his belt and tucked it into his own. He crossed over to Marshal and bent to the big man's feet.

"Don't even think of kicking me, Marshal," he warned before lifting the man's pant leg, exposing a switchblade harnessed to a strap around his thick, hairy calf.

"How did he know I had that?" Marshal asked Kyle in amazement, as Adam removed the deadly knife.

"What are you doing here?" Monique demanded.

"We're here to collect the interest you owe," Kyle answered.

"We already paid the interest," she countered.

Adam's mind raced to catch up with the situation at hand. He peered out the open window to the alley, where Marshal's Pontiac was parked directly below. He instantly recognized the suit pants in the passenger's seat to be his own. The plan was obviously still the same, or everything wouldn't have been progressing exactly as it had the first time. He thought back to the conversation he had with Kyle and Marshal in the Royal Cafe. They must have short-changed him on the payment, explaining Marshal's uneasiness and overzealous explanations at the meeting.

He quickly crossed to Kyle and roughly pulled back his

149

jacket and removed the ledger from his pocket. He opened it up and ran his finger down the list of names until he found Sinclair. In the adjacent column it read five thousand and under payments one thousand was scribbled.

"You double-crossing bastard," Adam said in a low contained voice. "You told me they only paid a thousand."

"What the hell are you talking about?" Kyle asked with a smirk.

"Claiborne," Adam hissed, remembering he would have to speak from Charlie's perspective. "You told him a thousand was paid on the debt! I gave you five. What did you do with the rest of it? Blow it up your nose?"

"He tacked on more interest, that's all," Kyle argued with amazing conviction.

"You stinking shit," Adam said, pushing the ledger into Kyle's chest. "I can't believe you expected to get away with this. Looks like we need to have a little chat with Mr. Claiborne to set him straight," he said, realizing the only way to settle it was to speak directly to himself.

Monique kept the gun leveled on the two men, ready to lead them downstairs, when she saw Amy teeter up behind Kyle. Her heart beat wildly upon seeing the small child within reach of the dangerous man. Kyle saw the panic on Monique's face and turned to see what was causing it.

"Amy, get out of here baby! Run!" Monique screamed, lunging for her child, but Kyle swooped the little toddler into his arms before Monique could stop him.

"What have we here?" he asked tossing the fragile child into the air.

"Kyle, put the baby down," Adam ordered.

Ignoring Adam's command, Kyle swirled with the terrified toddler out into the living room. He was now in complete control of the situation and was delighted with the power he held within his grasp. Monique, having abandoned the bulky shotgun to get to her child, raced into the living room after Kyle. Marshal saw the open opportunity and grabbed the weapon, just before Adam could grab it. He turned the shotgun around and butted him above the ear with the handle. Adam fell back in pain, the crack of the solid wood ringing through his skull.

Amy wailed out in screeching sobs of terror as the horrid, unfamiliar man continued to spin her. He moved carelessly about the room shattering vases and knocking over furniture, as Monique tugged at the child trying to pry her loose from his tight grip.

"Please, she's sick," she begged, but her pleading only seemed to entice Kyle more. Finally, she ran to the kitchen and grabbed a knife from a drawer and as soon as Kyle saw the blade, he stopped swirling and the smile disappeared from his face.

"Don't even think about it," he warned with a cold look of malice.

Monique instantly dropped the knife, as Marshal, having regained his handgun and the switchblade, pushed Adam into the living room, nudging him with the barrel of the shotgun. Adam had once again fallen victim to the weakness of Charlie's body. Any other time he could easily have overpowered the sluggish, bulky Marshal, but in Sinclair's shoes, he didn't stand a chance against the thug.

Amy's screams had subsided to a whimper, and except for the sound of the crying child, a tense silence filled the air. Monique flinched as Marshal carelessly tossed the loaded handgun to Kyle, who caught it with ease while holding Amy in the other hand.

"We don't have any more money," Monique said. "What the hell do you want?"

Kyle smiled at the question. "Just a few little errands. Mr.

151

Claiborne wants you to—"

"—do some pick-ups to pay off the money he thinks you owe," Adam finished for him, still breathing hard from the scuffle with Marshal. Kyle looked at him dumbfounded, unable to understand how he knew what he was going to say.

Kyle's stupid expression fueled Adam's anger. "Aside from stealing from me, you've got the cops on your stupid, bungling asses!" he exclaimed.

Kyle looked at Adam strangely, his attention so far shifted from the child in his arms that it appeared as though he were going to drop her. Monique started toward her, but Kyle saw her advancing and pulled back. "The baby stays with us," he said uneasily. Clearly, things weren't going as smoothly as he had anticipated.

"No, please," Monique begged.

The whole situation fell into place for Adam and he felt sick and disgusted with himself for being such a fool and going along with such a despicable scheme. "Kyle, you asshole! The child has asthma."

Kyle handed Amy to Marshal. "Get her out of here," he ordered.

Marshal stood awkwardly holding the squirming child. "What do I tell your brother?"

"Tell him the truth," Kyle ordered. "She's our collateral because they don't want to make good on their debt. You might also mention that they threatened to call the cops."

"That's a lie," Monique argued, though she knew it was in vain. Panic overtook her when Marshal carried the child toward the front door. "No!" she screamed, reaching for her baby.

Kyle raised his hand and slapped her across the face, sending her stumbling to the floor. Adam, at first disbelieving the assault, advanced toward Kyle. "You son-of-a-bitch," he bellowed.

152

Kyle shoved the pistol into his stomach. "Go ahead. I'd love to blow your guts out," he goaded.

Adam retreated, fully believing Kyle would pull the trigger if he were pushed. He felt ashamed at the sight of Monique's swelling jaw. He put his hand out to help her up, but she shunned his offer. It was clear that she considered him responsible for the injury and the last thing she wanted was his help. A look of resignation came across her face. She got to her feet and quickly grabbed a can of Proventil from the coffee table and held it out to Kyle.

"Sometimes she stops breathing. Just put it to her mouth and press," she instructed.

Kyle considered the canister held out to him.

"Please," Monique asked softly. "She could die without it."

Finally, to the mother's relief, Kyle snatched the medicine from her hand and slipped it into his pocket. "Get dressed," he ordered.

* * * * *

Claiborne glanced down at the tear-stained face of the wailing toddler who was sandwiched in the front seat between himself and Marshal. Her piercing screams bounced off the surrounding buildings which were so closely built to one another that no part of the cry seemed to escape the area. Claiborne looked over at Marshal with irritation, his scrutinizing eyes sending streams of sweat along the pudgy man's cheeks. "Couldn't you bozos have picked a more convenient piece of collateral?" he asked.

Marshal avoided his boss' eyes for fear if he looked into the brilliantly green irises they would scan his mind. "They didn't have anything else," he explained weakly.

Claiborne shook his head and turned back to watch the doorway in anticipation of Kyle and the others. He was angered that they even needed collateral to get the couple to cooperate. He was giving them another break by allowing them to work off their debt and when Marshal told him that they had refused and put up a fight, he felt betrayed once again by the unappreciative Sinclairs.

* * * * *

Inside the apartment, Adam's heart sank when Monique appeared from her bedroom wearing the same cotton dress that she was killed in. Just the sight of the colorful material brought back the nightmarish vision of her lying in the cellar with the bloodstained, muddy dress clinging to her dead body. Desperate to change anything possible about the recurring events, Adam thought momentarily about having her go back and put on different clothes, but Kyle quickly squelched the thought by yanking her toward the door.

"I can walk just fine, thank you," Monique said, pulling her arm from his grip.

"I get the feeling you don't like me," Kyle said in the sincerest voice he could muster. With the pistol resting in his palm, he motioned the couple toward the door. "Remember, don't try anything. Just get in your car and do as I told you," he ordered, pulling the door shut behind them.

Chapter 20

Dark thunderclouds promising rain loomed overhead, casting a murky, gray appearance to everything below. It was warm and deathly calm, giving a restless, dangerous feel to the air. When the trio exited into the alley, Monique quickly spotted Amy inside Marshal's car. A smile had replaced her daughter's tears and she was happily playing with some keys that Marshal dangled before her angelic face. Although Monique was relieved that her daughter was no longer frightened, the sight of her playing with such a vicious man sent a wave of fear crashing through her soul. The terror it evoked in her equaled that of a mother whose child was squatting beside an array of sweet, enticing honeysuckle vines, petting the pretty speckled scales of a rattlesnake perched in the shadows below. She wanted so badly to run to her rescue, but knew if she did the deadly fangs of the enemy could strike, sucking the life from the innocent, unsuspecting child.

Adam saw the terror, and gently placed his hands on her shoulders. "Why don't you let me drive?" he asked.

Although she surrendered the keys to him, finding slight reassurance in his soothing tone, she couldn't take her eyes off of her child. She knew she would eventually have to get into the old car, but at that moment, found it to be impossible. The passenger door next to her swung open from the inside.

"We have to go," Adam beckoned from the driver's seat.

She forced her stiff, yet shaking legs to obey, and lowered herself into the seat of the old Ford.

Kyle slammed the door behind her and tossed the ledger through her open window onto her lap. "Just follow the addresses and I'll be a happy man," he instructed, then headed back to join Marshal and Claiborne in the other car.

Monique's trembling hands leafed through the ledger to the beginning of the names. "Truman Nichols at 569 Decatur," she read aloud, her toneless voice sounding foreign to herself.

Adam put the coughing vehicle into gear and pulled out onto Dauphine Street. Accustomed to the control his own, newer car afforded, he was caught off guard by the old Ford's loose steering, which after a delayed reaction, swerved them to the left, nearly hitting the wall of a building. He was embarrassed by his awkward driving and looked to see if Monique noticed, but her attention was glued to Marshal's Pontiac that hung back a few hundred feet.

The French Quarter seemed deserted, with the exception of an occasional pedestrian in search of an early morning Bloody Mary. Tiny bits of trash, missed by the frequent street cleanings, began to tousle in the wind which was slowly and gradually picking up. After a few blocks, Adam made a turn onto Toulouse, this time compensating for the play in the wheel. They continued down the street, Monique waiting attentively for the Pontiac to also make the turn. "They're not behind us!" she cried after a moment.

"They know where we're going. They're just hanging back so it's not obvious that they're following us," Adam explained.

His words failed to comfort her and she grabbed the door handle as if to jump if he didn't obey her command. "Turn around," she said.

"Trust me, I've been through this," Adam said in a calm steady voice. "Everything is going just like it did before."

"Yeah, and we ended up dead!" she exclaimed.

"They'll be coming up that street any second," he reassured her, pointing to a side street ahead of them. Monique leaned back in anticipation, her hands tensely intertwined. Just as he had predicted, the shiny black nose of the Pontiac crept up into sight, rolling to a stop behind the intersection.

Monique looked over at Adam but instead of gratitude, her face imparted hatred. "Since this is your second time around, maybe you could tell me why you went along with kidnaping a sick baby," she said.

"I didn't know she was sick," he answered, thinking how ridiculously weak the excuse sounded.

"Oh, well, that's okay then," Monique retorted with sarcasm, then was silent for a moment. "You're a monster," she whispered, tears welling up in her eyes.

Adam sat helpless, knowing there was no way he could comfort her. Although he faced forward, he could see her biting back the tears and for the first time since he had inhabited Charlie's body, he felt sick to his stomach as acid began churning its way to his throat. He recognized the familiar burning and marveled that it had taken only a short while before the same bad habit of misdirecting stress attacked the perfectly healthy stomach of the body he now possessed.

* * * * *

They drove on in silence until he found the address of the exclusive restaurant located only a block away from historic

157

Jackson Square. Although Adam and his family frequented many expensive eateries, he had only been inside the restaurant once before and that was when he had made the actual loan to Truman Nichols. As with all of the loans he granted, he did the initial business of lending, and his brother and Marshal handled the task of collecting. Nichols had been loaned a very large sum of money and had yet to repay the remaining balance of thirty thousand which was nearly two months overdue. A week ago, he had actually considered calling on Nichols himself, but had yielded to Kyle's persuasion that he could handle the collection of the delinquent debt himself. If nothing else positive could be derived from the immediate situation, at least he could get some necessary business accomplished.

He flipped off the ignition, the engine of the old car protesting by sputtering a few times before giving way to silence. "Are you ready?" he asked Monique.

She nodded a silent "yes" and pushed open her squeaky door.

Marshal had parked the Pontiac half a block away, close enough for the men to observe the couple. They watched Adam start for the door of the restaurant, but to Claiborne's irritation, Monique hesitated outside of her car, staring down the street in their direction. A horse-drawn carriage full of early bird tourists passed by, momentarily blocking their view of her, but after the coach passed, she was still standing in the same spot.

"Oh, this is good," Claiborne mumbled. "If the cops are watching any of these places, they're going to wonder what the hell she's looking at."

Kyle reached for the door handle. "I'll take care of it," he offered. He stepped out onto the pavement and motioned down the street for Monique to go inside the restaurant. After a moment, she reluctantly turned in obedience.

* * * * *

"I'm sorry, sir, but we're closed until five o'clock," a tiny young hostess said, perched behind a podium with an artificial smile on her face. "Perhaps you would like a carry-out menu for later," she offered, inspecting their attire with disdain.

Even though Adam knew that they were poorly dressed and would normally agree with the acid-tongued snob, he felt a shot of anger. He glanced uneasily back at Monique, hoping the girl's hurtful remark had passed her by, but upon seeing her icy expression, he knew it hadn't. It was clear that she felt like slapping the girl, but instead held her beautiful head high with pride, returning the plastic courtesy.

"We're not here to eat, miss," Adam answered roughly. "We're here to speak with the owner."

"I'm afraid that's impossible," the hostess retorted.

Monique took a step forward. "It's concerning business with Mr. Nichols," she said. "And something tells me that he wouldn't appreciate you speaking to us in this manner," she said with such confidence that the girl dared not contest any further.

"Follow me," the hostess replied brusquely, before leading them through the doorway to the kitchen. As she pulled back the door, a myriad of sounds rushed upon them, revealing a whole life concealed behind the steel entrance.

Inside the large, immaculate kitchen, several chefs were busy preparing the night's feasts. Truman Nichols, a very large

159

hardy man in his fifties, was in the center of the room that was filled with steaming pots, stacked fruit, seafood and vegetables, and every kind of cutlery and kitchen accessories imaginable. His thick, white hair waved in all directions giving the impression of a mad man at work, while his deep gruff voice rose above the bustle to instruct the busy and obedient chefs. He plunged a long-handled spoon into a frothing kettle and pulled it back out to his full lips. The creator of the recipe stood motionless by, while his boss slurped the liquid like air into his mouth. After a tense moment, the brow of Nichols twisted into agony. "You call that bouillabaisse?" he bellowed in criticism, wiping his lips of the disappointment. "More shrimp and less pepper," he commanded.

The hostess gingerly approached the large man, minus the arrogance she had only moments earlier flaunted so openly.

"Mr. Nichols, there's a couple here to see you," she announced.

Nichols turned his red, hot face in her direction, ready to scream out for being interrupted by the girl, but upon seeing Monique, his expression softened. He put down the tasting spoon and waved for the hostess to disappear. She quickly obliged, brushing past the couple as if not to be forgotten so easily.

Nichols grunted a quick "Hello" to Adam, then feasted his eyes upon the delectable creature who stood before him, flashing her a grand smile.

Monique instantly liked the older man, feeling strangely comforted by his gallant strength, and couldn't resist returning the friendly, mischievous grin. He took her hand and bowed to kiss it. "May I be of service to you, Miss . . . ?"

"Sinclair," she answered with a smile.

160

"Miss Sinclair," he repeated, rolling the name across his tongue as if savoring a delicate wine.

Monique's heart lifted, feeling their task to be easier than she had anticipated. She shifted into gear and got down to business by immediately opening the ledger which she had brought from the car. Adam, having witnessed the exchange between Monique and the strong-willed man, decided it best to let her continue to handle the situation. "We're here on behalf of Adam Claiborne," Monique informed him.

Upon hearing the name Adam Claiborne, Nichols looked up at Adam with a little less friendliness. "Yes?" he asked.

Monique ran her finger along the line after Truman Nichols' name and was taken aback by the huge amount that was written below accounts receivable. "We're supposed to collect thirty-thousand dollars from you," she said somewhat uncertainly.

Nichols turned angrily toward Adam. "Is this some kind of a joke?"

Adam stood speechless, caught off guard by the sudden outburst. He was certain that the amount was correct, but turned to Monique who quickly double checked the sum.

"It says here thirty-thousand, due a month and a half ago," she said.

As if Adam were the one verifying the amount, Nichols grabbed him by the neck. "What the hell is this?" he demanded, a large vein bulging from his temple. Adam pried helplessly at the muscular fingers that squeezed so tightly that he was unable to breathe.

"That's what the book reads, Mr. Nichols," Monique quickly defended.

Adam looked wildly at Nichols, trying to speak, but the large hands pressed tighter around his only connection to air.

161

"Your books are wrong!" Nichols yelled. "I paid my loan two months ago!" And with his last statement, he threw Adam atop a steel table sending fruit flying everywhere. Adam lay gasping for air, and before he could get to his feet, Nichols continued with his assault. "I refuse to be harassed by you thugs any longer," he declared, pulling Adam off the table by his collar and throwing him past a couple of chefs who concentrated intensely on their work. "I have a respectable business here," Nichols bellowed, his large thighs booming in Adam's direction. Adam rolled to the side, but the huge hands rolled him back before belting him repeatedly in the face. The giant lifted him as if he were weightless and threw him into a bevy of pots and pans that went crashing to the colorful floor tiles. The worn material of Adam's shirt ripped open as Nichols grabbed him once again. "A loan does not constitute ownership, my friend," he said pounding him in the face before sending him flying into a stack of corn and carrots.

Just as Adam decided the attack had ended, he was drawn up like a puppet, his wooden legs dangling limp, his head thrust over a steaming pot. His face burned as he looked down at the boiling red crawfish sizzling inside.

"You tell Claiborne that if he sends another collector, especially a beautiful young woman, to do his dirty work, I'll boil him, butter him, and serve him as appetizer!" he heard the mammoth wail.

Suddenly, he was dropped in a heap onto the cold floor which offered relief from the hot steam. He turned onto his back ready for the attack to continue, but instead saw Nichols turn to Monique with a chivalrous smile.

"Would you relay that message for me, Miss Sinclair?" he asked sweetly.

Monique couldn't help but smile at the irony of the situation. "Consider it done," she replied.

Nichols took her by the hand. "Dinner on the house, any time my dear," he offered with a kiss. "Now if you'll excuse me please."

Nichols turned to leave as Adam picked himself up off the floor. "You're too skinny for this line of work," he whispered in Adam's direction as if letting him in on some great secret.

"I'll keep that in mind," Adam muttered to the passing man.

Monique tried to muffle her smile, clearly having enjoyed the event. "Mr. Nichols wanted me to tell you—"

"I heard," Adam interrupted, wincing in pain as he straightened his back.

"Are you gonna live?" she asked in a teasing tone.

"Yeah, but there isn't going to be anything left of your husband's body when I get through with it," he said inspecting his arms, already welting up with bruises.

The playfulness faded from Monique's demeanor as she weighed Adam's last words. "No there wasn't, was there?" she asked, remembering that Claiborne ended up killing him.

Adam looked up at her, realizing that what he said had been taken the wrong way.

"I know what you meant," she said as if reading his mind. "It looks like your brother is taking us all for a ride."

Adam didn't answer Monique's comment, only turned for the door. He felt more enraged at Kyle than he had ever remembered being. He couldn't understand what his brother had done with so much money. If Truman Nichols repaid his loan two months ago, there was no telling how long Kyle and Marshal had been stealing from him.

Chapter 21

Sheets of heavy rain cut down upon the pavement, sending gushing water along the sides of the street, rushing past the tires of Marshal's stationary Pontiac. Marshal flipped on the windshield wipers to clear away the blurred window, while Amy sat playfully babbling between him and Claiborne, Kyle leaning forward from the back seat. All of the men watched in anticipation for the couple to exit, Kyle and Marshal a little more anxiously than Claiborne. Between the flapping wipers, they saw the door to the restaurant suddenly swing open and Adam burst out onto the sidewalk, followed by Monique. It was obvious that Adam had taken a beating by the disheveled look of his torn clothes and his bruised face. Claiborne stiffened with concern. "Kyle, get out and see what happened," he ordered.

The couple was soaked by the drenching rain only seconds after stepping onto the street. Adam angrily turned in the direction of Marshal's Pontiac, bent on setting things straight and doing a little pounding of his own on his irresponsible, dishonest brother. He wasn't surprised when Kyle got out of the car and headed toward him and Monique. What did surprise him though, was the sight of Marshal's switchblade cuffed inside of Kyle's sleeve, hidden from sight of the Pontiac, but pointed straight at himself. Before he could react, Kyle had him by the arm with the knife pressed into his gut, the blade so close he felt the stinging metal slice into his skin.

Rain sprayed down Kyle's dark face, making his skin appear almost liquid. "Get back in your car and continue on the rounds," he shouted above the downpour.

"You've already made the rounds!" Adam exclaimed.

From the shelter of the Pontiac, Claiborne and Marshal observed the seemingly normal conversation, with Adam's unhappy face the only sign of friction.

"He looks pissed," Claiborne noticed.

Marshal cracked his window to let a little air into the stuffy, humid car, then picked Amy up into his lap.

"We're not going to be your stool pigeons, you double-crossing bastard!" Adam shouted at Kyle, their noses nearly touching.

Monique nervously looked toward the Pontiac, fearing for her daughter's safety during the heated argument. Through the rain she could see Marshal raise her child to the driver's window and wave the baby's arm "Hi" to her. Marshal's grave smile offered a sharp contrast to the baby's sparkling giggle. Monique felt her knees go weak and took Adam's hand to steady herself. "Let's just do what he says," she asked, tugging at Adam to back off. He reluctantly pulled away from Kyle, who retracted the switchblade into its casing.

Adam looked toward the Pontiac where Marshal was still holding up the child. He hadn't realized it the first time, but Marshal was threatening the child's safety right before his very eyes, only this time he had the perspective to understand it. He looked at Kyle. "You tell Marshal that if he touches that baby, I'll kill him, personally."

* * * * *

165

Kyle stood motionless until the couple was back in the confines of their own vehicle. He quickly tried to come up with an explanation for his brother who was waiting for his return.

"Well?" Claiborne asked, after Kyle had settled into the back seat and slammed the door against the noisy storm.

"He said they got the thirty thousand, but he had to beat it out of him," Kyle replied.

Claiborne looked around in amazement at the idea of the scrawny little Sinclair, beating up the huge Nichols. "What do you know about that," he mused trying to picture the unlikely scene. "Hmm," he said, digesting the bizarre thought. "They're working out better than I thought," he finally concluded and signaled for Marshal to start the car.

* * * * *

Water dripped from Monique's sodden hair, blurring the ink of the next name on the open ledger, but luckily she was still able to make out the letters. "Cora Bellfont," she read aloud. "The Tenth Ward." She looked incredulously over at Adam. "That's a slum."

Adam felt as if he were getting it from all sides. "I give them loans when no one else will touch them," he defended.

"Interest free?" she quipped.

Adam didn't answer, he just put the sinking car into gear and pulled slowly away from the river that had swallowed the curb. He had always thought of himself as a good man, but suddenly everything he had done seemed evil with ill-fated intentions that he didn't recall having at the time.

He remembered the day he had loaned Cora the two-thou-

166

sand dollars. He didn't haggle with her for references or even collateral like he demanded from so many others, or like any legitimate loaning institution would have; instead, he saw that she needed the money and trusted she would repay it. He felt as though he did the right thing, but had the extra fee really been necessary? Yes, he decided. How could he make a profit without fees? Truly some of his judgments were misguided and perhaps nearsighted, but he had the right to earn a living.

Chapter 22

As they left the French Quarter and the surrounding downtown area, the rain stopped so abruptly that it was as if someone in the heavens had turned off a faucet. By the time they reached the Tenth Ward, which was only ten minutes away, the sun was beating down upon the puddles, brewing up a steamy afternoon. The houses along Cora's street were built so closely together that the decaying structures leaned against one another, threatening to crush the next if it showed any sign of weakness. Black children, and an occasional white, played in the streets, their own tiny yards filled with rusted skeletons of cars and every other imaginable piece of garbage. Elderly men and women stood against the houses chatting with one another, deprived of the luxury of a shady tree. Laundry, soaked from the previous rain, hung limply from wires sporadically stretched between wayward nails. Although Monique's old car was right at home in the slum, the new Pontiac which followed it stuck out like a red siren. Marshal drove in a steady slow pace, the children staring while they slowly parted for its path.

With Monique's help, Adam found Cora's address and cut the engine; this time he was almost grateful for the sputtering carburetor. The house before them was so narrow in width that the space between the outer side walls only allowed for a front door and no windows, giving the home a surreal appearance. As they sat in silence, Adam saw the disgust in Monique's eyes.

"When I loaned her the money, she didn't tell me she was this poor," he explained. "She came to my office and I didn't see where she lived."

"Yeah, but you knew when you came to collect," Monique argued.

Adam glanced at the Pontiac in his rear-view mirror. He could see himself in the seat beside Marshal, staring ahead, not looking at the surrounding poverty. She was right, he could have stopped the collection. At least the interest, anyway.

"I have to feed my family, too, you know," he defended to Monique. She glanced over at him in disbelief.

"You're joking, right?" she asked.

Anger shot through Adam. He was tired of defending himself to the woman, and to himself. He abruptly opened his car door.

The couple mounted the step to the house which was raised on pilings, a necessary practice to keep the impending threat of floods from destroying their homes.

Stomach acid stung through Adam's throat as he rested his eyes upon the screen door hanging weakly by its hinges. Fearing that if he knocked on the fragilely suspended door it might fall off, he opted instead to tap on the door casing. Monique stood beside him, her mouth set in silence, refusing him idle conversation. Through the hole-filled screen, he could see a baby girl playing within the dark boxy room that resembled a closet more than a living room. "Hello?" Monique called out gently, eager to get the business over and done with. After several calls, an extremely thin figure finally came out of the darkness. It was Cora Bellfont, appearing much more fragile than Adam had remembered her. She graciously opened the door, wiping her forehead with her dirty apron.

"Well, hello there. Sorry I didn't hear you at first," she apologized through a nearly toothless smile. "Good Lord, it's hot," she sighed, her friendly small eyes resembling acorns.

Monique smiled with apprehension. "Yeah, it sure is, Ma'am."

"How can I help you?" Cora asked.

Adam stepped forward. "We're here on behalf of Adam Claiborne to pick up some money," he informed her.

The smile immediately left the woman's face as she stepped back from the door. "Just a moment," she said weakly.

She disappeared inside of the dark house and less than a minute later, she returned with a roll of bills bound in a rubber band. This time, she stayed behind the screen and handed the money through the slightly cracked door. Neither of the two reached for the money, until finally Monique glanced over at Adam. He reluctantly reached out and took the money from Cora's hand.

"Please tell Mr. Claiborne that I can't keep paying his so-called interest. I'm not a rich woman, as you can see," she said.

"You've already repaid your loan?" Adam asked, a pit in his stomach joining the acid.

"Time and time again," she answered. "He may be rich, but he sure ain't honorable."

Adam unclenched his sweaty hand, revealing the crinkled bills for Cora to reclaim. "I promise, no one will be back to collect from you."

Cora hesitated as if the money were poison. "Please, mister. I don't want no more trouble," she said through a cracking voice.

"There won't be. I promise," he reassured her, pressing the money into the palm of her bony hand.

"We're very sorry, Ms. Bellfont," Monique said, before following Adam back to the car.

Chapter 23

Briggs watched with increasing despair as the sun disappeared behind Kyle's apartment building, slowly immersing the city into night. Although he and Detective Hays had been on duty for nearly twenty-six hours, the sergeant had refused to answer their calls for relief detectives. Apparently their superior had no intention of letting them off the assignment so easily when they had screwed it up so badly the first time around. With the daylight dwindling, Briggs resigned to the fact he would have to wait until the next morning to drive back out to the West Bank for his lost watch.

"Do you want to go or should I?" his partner asked, breaking the extended silence.

"I'll go," Briggs volunteered. Anything to escape the gnawing pain in his hind quarters caused by sitting for hours on end. "Burgers or tacos?" he asked.

"You decide," Hays said without enthusiasm. Clearly, he didn't feel like having the same discussion for the third time that day. He, too, had the look of a ragged dog after a long run. The only difference was that he and Briggs hadn't been running: they had been sitting still in the same spot for almost twenty-one hours of the long shift. Religiously they had watched Kyle's apartment building, waiting for any sign of movement from within, but there had been none since four that morning when Kyle had stumbled in.

"Don't go to sleep," Briggs warned before stepping from the car, sending his back into a popping frenzy. "I'll be back in a few minutes," and he took out on foot in the opposite direction from the apartment building.

Chapter 24

Adam and Monique exited a French bakery, once again without any money to show for the stop. Even though they were both relieved that the scorching sun had been replaced with the cool blue moon, it offered little relief from the misery the sweltering day had inflicted upon them. The heat combined with their anxiety, had gradually sucked their energy dry. They went from address to address, trying to collect what had already been taken, the Pontiac looming behind like a dark shadow. Even though they hadn't collected a cent all day, they had no other choice than to cooperate with Kyle's ridiculous scheme by continuing on the rounds like actors playing out a farce. Every time Adam tried to get close to the Pontiac to explain to himself the deceitful facade, Marshal would inadvertently threaten Amy. Although he had never known Kyle to harm a child, he wasn't sure of anything concerning his brother any more and he certainly wasn't sure of the depth of Marshal's maliciousness. For fear of the child's safety, he was forced time and time again to retreat to the car with Monique.

Adam seated himself again behind the wheel, despair filling his heart as he waited for Monique to read the next name. He had been unsuccessful in changing the course of events, and if everything kept going as it was, he and Monique would be dead in less than eight hours. He wiped the sweat from his brow, deciding that as soon as he got the chance, he would go to St. Mary's and speak with Father Jacob. Surely by that time he would have arrived to replace Father Paul, and he would be able to reconfess his sins.

"I thought you were scared of voodoo," Monique said.

"What do you mean?" Adam muttered, drawn from his thoughts by the strange comment.

"Madame Peppy is next," she answered, the open ledger resting in her lap. "She's one of the most famous Priestesses around."

"She told me she ran a gift shop."

"She does, voodoo gifts," Monique said with a laugh.

Adam couldn't help but smile. "So where is it?"

"Four Hundred Saint Ann Street," she noted.

Adam put the car into gear and pulled away from the curb. He drove in silence, the tightness returning to his chest. He thought of the feeble child, who would end up dead if he couldn't somehow reverse the course of time. Although he was still unsure how the child had died, he knew in his heart that if he hadn't have killed her parents, they would have been there to save her. How had he spun such an evil trap for himself? What was the purpose of him going back in time, if everything were just going to repeat itself? Sweat blurred his vision as he tried to focus on the steamy pavement ahead.

"Thank you," Monique said quietly.

"What for?" Adam asked.

"For helping me protect my baby."

"Yeah. A real good guy, huh?"

"Underneath it all, yes," she answered much to his surprise. "I just don't think you know that." Monique had seen through-out the day, the diligence with which Adam had cooperated with his brother in order to protect her child. She also saw beneath

175

the tough exterior to the pain that was eating away at his gut. "I think you judge yourself and everyone else so harshly that it's impossible to live up to your expectations. You only see the world in black and white and no shades of gray. Unfortunately, people fall into the gray category, including myself," she stressed looking over at him. "When I slept with you, I told myself that the only reason I was doing it was to help my baby, but then when I enjoyed it, as you said," she smiled, "I knew that my baby wasn't the only reason I had done it. I was attracted to you."

Adam looked up. He had never thought for even one second that she found anything about him appealing.

"You were so strong and knew what you wanted," she continued wistfully staring out the window. "I hated myself for being so weak and hiding my weakness behind supposed strength. It wasn't until Charlie forgave me that I forgave myself."

"He knew?" Adam asked.

"He didn't say anything, but he knew. Charlie's an incredible man. He knows my faults and still grants me unconditional love . . . love I don't always deserve. I love Charlie deeply, but I'm not in love with him, I never have been," Monique said. "He knows that but accepts me anyway."

"Then why did you marry him?"

"When I met Charlie I was eight months pregnant with Amy and I was feeling terribly guilty for bringing a little child into the world without a father to love it. I was raised without the benefit of a mother and I always swore to myself that my children would have two parents instead of one. Charlie came along and taught me that I could forgive myself. That the world wasn't black and white and didn't always work out the way my analytical controlling mind wanted. We became great friends, and I knew he would be a wonderful husband and father. That's why I married him. I've been very happy with Charlie and I couldn't possibly find better, but there's always been a void. When I met you, you aroused something in me that I thought had withered away. It was the only time I ever cheated on him, and it'll be the last. I broke a bond between me and Charlie that'll never be the same. The only way to even come close to mending it is by remembering what I've got and protecting it. I'm not perfect," she said turning her eyes upon Adam. His heart faltered at her gaze. "No one is," she concluded sadly, then rested her head back on the seat. The remainder of the ride was spent in silence.

* * * * *

A large, wood slatted porch with a covered sidewalk shaded the entrance like the old storefronts of western towns. Adam stopped the car in front of the door, verifying the address to be four hundred Saint Ann. A sign, suspended overhead by two rusty chains, creaked slowly in the breeze, the words . . . "HOUSE OF VOODOO SINCE 1912" . . . branded into the rotted wood.

Bells jingled to announce their entrance into the small room which resembled an old cabin. The door clanged shut behind them, enclosing the couple within the warm, colorful interior, its floors and walls built of cypress wood. The pungent scent of incense rushed through Adam's nostrils and mouth, scratching his throat with every breath he inhaled. Alligator claws were abundantly draped about the window, black voodoo dolls, made of Spanish moss wrapped in brilliant cloth, hung from nails tacked to the walls. An oil painting of the famous Marie Louvou hung above a mantel, beneath it a stack of alligator and snake heads.

177

Rastifarian music was playing so clearly that it seemed as though the musicians were in the very room with them. "You call this normal?" Adam asked in amazement of the eccentric dwellings.

"I never said it was normal," Monique smiled. "Or even sane. But hey, you got to believe in something, right?"

Adam had to smile. Although he still thought the place ridiculous, she did have a point. He supposed that his beliefs, which he clung so blindly to, probably seemed just as strange to her.

Business was being tended to by a young, overweight girl who stood behind a glass counter, taking samples from various clear jars filled with herbs and nutria and placing them into a small bag. Her extremely short cropped hair and dark clothing, complete with army boots, gave her a very harsh appearance. Her multi-pierced ears were adorned with charms and trinkets, some of which hung clear to her shoulders. The young clerk's radical appearance seemed to go unnoticed by her two customers: an elderly couple dressed straight out of Sears and Roebuck. They waited patiently while she compiled the assortment of remedies into what she referred to as a "Gris Gris" Bag. The sight of the conservative couple in such an unlikely place struck Adam as the oddest thing of all.

"Excuse me, miss," he interrupted.

When the girl looked up at him, he was taken aback by her beautiful eyes, which instantly softened her appearance. Their warm, green tone laced with gold, combined with her light brown complexion, bespoke of her mulatto blood.

"Yes?" she asked kindly.

"We're here to collect for Adam Claiborne," he said, almost frightened to speak the name in the foreign place after the awful reactions it had been evoking all day. Much to his and Monique's surprise, the young girl smiled.

"We were wondering about that," she laughed. "Let me get my Granny," she offered before disappearing through a curtain to a connecting room.

Abandoned at the counter, the elderly couple spoke quietly between one another trying to decide which of the herbs were best for their needs. The husband wanted something for his arthritis—which the rainy weather of the South irritated—while the wife thought he would be better off addressing the issue of his hot temper. The husband flared at the suggestion and after a few heated whispers, they too were waiting in silence along with Monique and Adam.

Within a minute, Madame Peppy appeared through the curtain, her granddaughter close behind. The old woman had long, ratty hair, held back with a brightly colored head band containing every color of the rainbow. Multiple strands of spirit beads dangled from her long wrinkled neck, laying across her ample bosom she displayed proudly. The ancient woman reminded Adam of a crinkled turtle smiling at him past toothless gums.

"I thought you would never come," she laughed, holding out a small bag that jingled of money.

The couple stood speechless, stunned by the unexpected, kind reception.

"You youngins' don't look the part of thugs," the old woman cackled with laughter. "Now that Kyle is a different story. I've never seen such an ornery fellow . . . and superstitious! Why he got one look at Betsy and turned white as a sack of flour. He backed out the door so fast I couldn't get the money into his hand. And far be it from me to force money on anyone," she laughed.

179

Just then Adam saw a large snake slither out of the other room and curl behind the counter.

"Betsy," the granddaughter said in irritation. "Get off my feet."

No further explanation was necessary for Adam or Monique who chuckled over the amusing thought of Kyle racing from the store, terrified of the toothless woman and her harmless snake. It was the first pick-up of the day that hadn't already been collected and now they knew why. Kyle was too scared to step his greedy feet back into the store. "Thank you," Adam said, shaking his head.

"Good bye," Monique said sweetly to the old woman, then turned to leave.

"No, not yet," Madame Peppy called out, rushing behind a counter filled with assorted hand painted jewelry. "You two need protection if you're going to be hanging out with the likes of that other fellow. He's got a dark side to him." She grabbed a trinket from a basket and hobbled back over to the couple. "May I?" she asked Monique, referring to the chain containing the locket.

Monique looked at Adam uncertainly.

"Sure," she said finally, removing the chain from her neck.

"He said he was Catholic so I'm giving you a talisman a Catholic will respect," the old woman said as she opened the clasp of the necklace.

She placed the trinket on the chain, and to Adam's horror, when it dropped alongside the locket, he saw that it was the hand-painted Saint Christopher's medal that had fallen from Charlie's body.

"A Saint Christopher's medal," Monique said aloud, realizing that it was the same one that Adam had spoken of.

"The saint of protection," the old woman said, as she held it out ready to place it back around Monique's neck. "No," she said, stopping in mid air. The smile left her crinkled old face as she turned gravely to Adam. "You need it more," and she put it around his neck.

The couple was stunned that another link in the chain of events had fallen into place. Although Adam had already accurately foretold various events of the day, Monique found the unfolding of this prediction the most disconcerting of all. It had seemed most unlikely and yet had come true in the strangest of ways. Terror ripped through her at the thought of her own death which seemed for the first time to be inevitable and inescapable.

"I need to go," she said faintly, sweat forming on her upper lip.

Adam noticed the sudden paleness of her complexion and wondered if she was going to be sick. He took her gently by the arm and led her to the door.

Once outside, the night air helped her to regain her composure. When she turned to Adam under the street light, he saw the dark circles that were beginning to appear beneath her eyes. She was tired and frightened.

"It's happening, isn't it?" she asked.

"We can still stop it," he said, trying his best to sound convincing.

"My baby. You never said what happens to her," she whispered.

"It'll be all right," he answered. "We'll finish the rounds, then I'll go see the priest."

A glimmer of hope flickered across the worried mother's face.

181

Chapter 25

When Adam and Monique stepped out into the street to get into their car, the headlights of the Pontiac automatically flipped on. The couple was instantly illuminated like two helpless victims stalked by a relentless phantom that hung back in the night watching their every move. Monique turned into the light to check on her baby, but the powerful beams blinded her from seeing the car's passengers. Adam opened the door for her then cut across the front of the car and got behind the wheel. He put the keys in the ignition, as Monique opened the ledger for the last collection. Suddenly he heard a gasp. Monique was staring down at the ledger in disbelief.

"What is it?" he asked.

"Wilton Young," she read aloud then looked up at him with frightened eyes.

"Your father?" he muttered, disbelieving that the old man's name could be on the list.

"That must be how he broke his wrist and his ribs," she said, concluding that the elderly man's frequent injuries were no accidents after all. Throughout the day, she had witnessed the aftermath of Kyle and Marshal's harsh tactics in collecting the loans. She saw the bruises and fear-stricken faces, that hid behind the safety of their screen doors. "Oh God, how could I be so stupid?

He's not a rich man! I should have known when he offered us the money," she cried. "I didn't even question where he got it, I just assumed it was from his savings."

"You couldn't have known," Adam said, trying to protect her from her own self incrimination.

Monique turned on him. "But you knew! Why didn't you tell me Wilton borrowed money from you?"

"He didn't," Adam replied. "I never even spoke to him until last night."

"Then how do you explain this?" she demanded, holding up the ledger.

"I don't know," he answered, then he remembered that Wilton had mentioned Kyle's name the previous night. "He must have gotten the loan directly from Kyle. Kyle's probably trying to go out on his own."

"But how would he know Kyle and not you?" she asked. Then, as if suddenly realizing the answer herself, she sighed heavily. "Oh, God" she said. "Kyle came to the club a couple of weeks ago to collect from us when Wilton was there. He must have seen Kyle giving Charlie a hard time out back."

Her face was suddenly illuminated by the headlights of the Pontiac flashing on and off behind them.

"What are we supposed to do?" she asked, looking anxiously around at the waiting car. "I can't collect from Wilton. I know he doesn't have the money. He gave it all to me last night."

Adam started the old engine. "We better go through the motions, anyway," he said and pulled away from the curb.

*　*　*　*　*

183

The old car, with the ever present Pontiac in tow, cut through the narrow streets of the French Quarter toward Monique's apartment building.

Behind the wheel, Adam tried to ignore the invading guilt that was playing upon his conscience. He knew he was partially to blame for Wilton's broken bones and for the gruesome gash that the old man had tried so desperately to hide from Monique. Adam shook his head in disgust at the thought of Kyle beating the elderly man for not meeting his payment schedule. How could his brother be so ruthlessly ignorant? By breaking the old man's wrist, he had only compounded the problem. He had rendered the musician unable to play the trumpet, therefore unable to earn a living. Adam was sickened by the vicious cycle he himself had set into motion. He looked over at Monique, who sat silently, with her hands clenched tightly to one another, her eyes focused on the street ahead. He wanted to make everything right again: to go back to the beginning and stop the pain and misery he had bestowed upon the once happy family. Unfortunately though, he hadn't been sent far enough back in time to correct the damage that had already been done.

As the old car rounded the corner of Monique's street, they heard the wail of an ambulance coming from the opposite end of the block in their direction. Adam pulled the car to the side expecting the ambulance to continue on past, but instead, it stopped abruptly in front of Monique's apartment.

"That's my building," Monique said, leaning uneasily forward in her seat.

Adam pulled away from the curb and as they drew nearer, Monique froze at the sight of her boss, Jimmy, standing in the middle of the street. He was directing the paramedics who were busy removing an empty stretcher from the back of the ambulance.

"Hurry!" she cried to Adam who immediately sped up. Before the car came to a complete halt, Monique jumped from the passenger door, nearly stumbling to the ground.

"Is it Wilton?!" she exclaimed, running up to the distressed looking Jimmy, who immediately took her hands into his own.

Jimmy looked at her with painful eyes. "I came by to see why he wasn't at the poker game," he said weakly. "In ten years, he's never missed —"

Monique didn't wait for him to finish. She broke loose from his grip and raced for the door.

"Don't go up there, Moon!" he called out, running after her.

Although Adam was close behind, he would have given anything not to enter the building. The heavy weight of fear pulled at his ankles as dread descended upon his shoulders. Dread that he would somehow be responsible for the tragedy unfolding before him.

* * * * *

The dingy walls of the dark hallway seemed to be growing longer, taunting Monique against reaching Wilton's apartment. She sprinted as fast as her legs would carry her for what seemed like an eternity.

"Wilton?" she called out, his doorway finally appearing at the end of the hall.

Monique shoved the door aside and disappeared into the dark seemingly abandoned apartment. She went quickly to the living room and switched on the lamp. "Wilton?" she called out, but he was no where to be seen. She turned toward his bedroom, Adam and Jimmy quickly behind her.

"Moon, please!" Jimmy begged.

Wilton's bedroom was dark, except for a red neon sign which shone eerily through the window affording enough light for clear visibility. When Monique entered the doorway, she instantly spotted Wilton on the bed, lying with his back to the door, curled up in a fetal position. "Wilton?" she whispered. With her eyes fixed upon him, she moved slowly to the other side of the room, her body taking her without command. As she rounded the foot of the bed, she could see that his skin had been drained of all color, making him appear to be much older, his feeble body withered and thin.

"Oh my God," she faltered.

Adam was frozen by the tragic sight, as Monique descended upon the motionless Wilton and began shaking him. "Papa!" she cried out, but he didn't respond. She lunged to her knees and frantically reached beneath the bed, grasping blindly for Wilton's medical bag. Finally her hand landed on the leather case. She ripped it open and turned it upside down, dumping the contents onto the floor, bottles and bandages scattering everywhere.

"He needs insulin!" she screamed, rummaging through the paraphernalia.

"We're too late," Adam said gently, recognizing the stillness of death.

Jimmy looked away, unable to bear the sight.

Monique turned to Wilton with tears streaming down her face. "You're not going to do this," she said with dark determination, as she grasped a needle and quickly and expertly filled it with insulin. She reached for Wilton's arm and as she pulled up his sleeve, her hand touched the cold waxy skin that once had felt warm and full of life. Terror wrenched the breath from her lungs as she fell slightly back, the icy sensation of his skin burning into her fingertips. With all of her might, she raised the increasingly heavy needle to his arm, but her vision was blurred by the streaming tears. She angrily wiped them away and placed the tip of the needle once again to his skin, but her shaking hands betrayed her and the needle clinked across the floor. The room was silent except for her own heavy breathing as she knelt beside the bed, terrified of looking into her father's face. Her eyes slowly moved up to the sunken flesh that had been transformed into something so foreign that the face appeared her enemy. Death had reaped his soul, leaving behind a shell so alien and void that the image would haunt her for the rest of her life. She bent over the cold body, searching for the father she had cherished for thirty years. "Papa," she whispered, but there was no glimpse of him behind the darkened eye sockets. Wrapping her arms around the dead man's neck, she held him tight, refusing to accept the cruel finality of death. "Papa, Papa," she cried softly, thinking if she concentrated hard enough Wilton would come back like he always had.

A paramedic touched her shoulder. "Ma'am . . . " he said but her cries became more frantic. "Ma'am . . . " he repeated, finally breaking through her mounting hysteria. She suddenly stopped and looked up at him in silence.

She saw the paramedics, Jimmy and Adam all crowded into the tiny doorway looking at her. Her eyes turned to Adam, who was the only one she wanted to comfort her.

Adam saw the need and went to her. He was moved by the little girl that shone through her grief stricken eyes which were

187

swollen and red. He brushed the hair from her face and took her into his arms. She felt so soft and helpless as she leaned into him. Her body began to tremble and the tears came rushing back.

"Why?" she sobbed, holding onto him desperately.

Adam held her tight, his own throat clenching back the tears.

"Come on," Jimmy said gingerly to the couple. "Let's go in the other room.

Adam kept his arm around Monique and he led her through the living room into the kitchen. Jimmy flipped on the light that hung over the table as Adam pulled out a chair for Monique to sit in. Adam went to the sink and wet a rag with cool water. Jimmy stood next to Monique as Adam sat down in front of her and began gently wiping her tears away with the soothing cloth.

"Why?" she whispered, looking up at Jimmy. "Wilton's been diabetic for years. He's never missed his medicine."

Jimmy stared down at her a moment, his brow furrowed into several deep creases.

"Jimmy?" she asked, seeing that he knew more than he was saying.

"Wilton asked me to never tell you this, but I think I'm going to have to," he confided with great difficulty. "He called me last night. He wanted to borrow some money. He said that he had gotten into bad debt and needed some money by today."

Adam put his head in his hands; he didn't want to hear the forthcoming information.

"I told him that I didn't have it," Jimmy continued, "and I don't," he quickly added. "Well, when Wilton heard that I couldn't loan him the money, he said not to worry. That he had a savings account that he could dip into. I swear I had no idea he was talking about committing suicide to get to it."

Monique looked at him strangely. "Suicide?" she asked.

"I found this when I found him," Jimmy said, holding up two envelopes. "One is a life insurance policy."

"Oh God," Monique quavered, taking the envelopes from his hand. She stared down at the smaller of the two envelopes. It was in Wilton's finest stationery and addressed to her. She slowly ripped it open, careful not to damage the contents.

She instantly recognized Wilton's awkward handwriting etched shakily across the page. She read the words aloud for fear if she didn't they would slip from her unsteady grasp.

"Dear Moon," she started with great apprehension. "I've gotten into a rough spot that I can't seem to get out of, and I'm afraid that if I don't clear things up, you and Amy might get hurt. I've lived a long happy life and it's time for me to move on. I have a life insurance policy that will be enough money to clear my debt and to take care of you and Amy for a long time. Being as sick as I am, it was only a matter of time, anyway. I love you with all my heart . . . " she read, the tears again flooding her eyes. "Forgive me . . . Wilton."

There was silence as Monique rubbed at her eyes, trying to stop the stubborn tears. After a moment, she looked up at Adam, who expected her to lash out at him, but instead there was no anger in her eyes, only sorrow.

"We could have gotten the money some other way," she said softly.

"Excuse me," a man's voice interrupted. A paramedic was standing in the doorway. "Where would you like me to take the body?" he asked.

Monique was momentarily stunned by the question and she struggled with an answer. "I . . . can't . . . I," she stammered.

"I'll take care of it, love," Jimmy said, then turned to the young man. "I'll be out in a second."

"We've got to go," Monique abruptly announced, standing to her feet.

Jimmy turned back to her with grave concern. "Where are you going?"

"Please, Jimmy," she said. "Please take care of things. I'll be back later."

"Okay," he agreed quietly, his round little face scrunching in worry. "Are you going to be okay?"

"Yeah," she said steadily. "We just have to go pick up Amy."

Chapter 26

The Pontiac was parked in front of a beer tavern halfway down the street from the apartment building. In spite of the pounding bass emanating from the tavern, Amy and Marshal dozed comfortably next to one another, drool dribbling out of the corner of Marshal's mouth. Claiborne kept his eyes on the apartment building, while Kyle punched numbers into a small calculator in the back seat.

"What do you think is going on?" Claiborne asked, annoyed that the ambulance was blocking his view to the main entrance of the building.

"Some old geezer probably kicked the bucket," Kyle said.

"What's the total?" Claiborne asked.

"Well, there's thirty thousand from Truman Nichols, along with all these others. It adds up to fifty-two thousand, on the nose," he replied. After adding all the figures of what should have been collected, Kyle was amazed at the staggering amount he had spent on cocaine.

"When they come out, collect the money," Claiborne ordered.

From the front seat, Claiborne couldn't see the impact his instructions had on his brother seated in the shadows behind him. Kyle chewed nervously on the pencil eraser wondering what in the hell he would do when the couple came out. He had engineered the whole set up so perfectly, but had neglected to figure out how to tie it up. As he tried desperately to devise a plan, the couple exited the building before he reached a solution.

"There they are," Claiborne announced, eager to receive his money.

Kyle jumped from the car and walked as quickly as he could in the couple's direction. He was irritated at his brother for putting him in such an awkward situation. If he wasn't so damn eager to collect his money, he would have had more time to come up with a viable plan. As he drew near the couple, standing outside of their car, he saw that Monique had been crying.

"Have a good day?" he asked with a smile.

"You piece of shit," Monique said bitterly, then spit into his smirking face.

With a slow steady hand, Kyle wiped the moisture from his stubbled cheek, then pulled back his hand to strike her. Adam saw the intention in his brother's eyes and quickly grabbed his hand and threw a punch to his stomach.

From the Pontiac, Claiborne saw his brother double over in pain. "What the hell is going on out there?" he demanded, rousing Marshal from his cat nap. Marshal drew to attention quickly when he realized that trouble was at hand.

"Get out and tell Sinclair to come over here," Claiborne ordered.

Marshal became alarmed at his boss' request and instead of obeying, sat motionless in his seat. Claiborne turned on him in a fury. "Get out you dumb ass and call him over here," he repeated.

Marshal reluctantly obeyed and just as the sole of his shoe hit the pavement, a police car rounded the corner. Upon seeing the cop, he pulled his leg back inside and started the car.

"What in God's name are you doing?" Claiborne demanded.

"There's a cop," Marshal pointed out. Although he knew that the policeman was probably on routine surveillance, he decided to use the cop's presence as the perfect scapegoat.

At the sound of the starting engine, Monique saw that the Pontiac was headed toward them. She ran to the center of the street just as the car passed with her child inside.

"They're leaving!" she shrieked at the sight of the disappearing tail-lights.

Adam managed to wrangle free from Kyle's tight grasp and tore out running toward the Pontiac. "Kyle's ripping you off! The people already paid!" he screamed but was too late, the tail-lights were merely two red dots in the distance.

While Monique and Adam's attention was on the passing Pontiac, Kyle grabbed a taxicab that was waiting at the Grand Royal Hotel across the street. He rushed up to the passenger door, shoving a middle-aged business man out of the way.

"Hey you asshole," the man disputed, the contents of his brief case strewn across the sidewalk.

"Find another," Kyle threatened, slamming the door in his face.

"Get moving, mister," he ordered the driver, pointing to the direction in which the Pontiac had disappeared. With luck on his side, he would be able to catch it and explain to his brother what had happened before the Sinclairs had a chance to tell their side of the story.

"Kyle, you son-of-a-bitch!" Adam yelled as the taxicab flew by him and Monique.

Monique ran to her own car, her only thoughts were of saving her baby. She checked the ignition but the keys were missing.

193

"Give me the keys," she called out to Adam from behind the wheel. Instead of giving them to her he opened her door. "Scoot over . . . I know where they're going," he asserted.

Monique reluctantly slid over in the seat, and Adam took her place as driver. He started the car and headed in the direction of the fleeing taxicab and Pontiac.

"What are they going to do with my baby?" she cried as Adam maneuvered the old car past a busy intersection, horns blaring and tires screeching.

"Nothing yet," he promised, daring not to look away from the darting road, the bumper of the taxicab within an arm's reach.

Suddenly the taxicab made a sharp right and Adam swerved the old car around so as not to rear end it. Monique looked back at the yellow cab which was quickly disappearing into the night.

"What are you doing?" she asked in alarm. "He turned!"

"We'll catch up to them later."

"Are you crazy?" she cried. "That's my baby they've got!"

"I already know where they're taking her. They're going to my house," he said with complete conviction.

"So go there, then," she urged.

Adam looked her straight in the eyes. "Look, this is all happening just like it did before and unless we do something different, we're going to end up dead."

"Deserting my baby is not the answer," she bristled.

"Your baby will be fine until we get there," he reassured her. "But first, I need to make another stop." He gripped the wheel in frustration. "No matter how hard I try to change the events, everything we do is exactly what you and your husband did the first time around." She could see the fright in his eyes and it gave her a chill. "I don't know how to change things," he admitted, "but I know someone who might."

194

Chapter 27

Adam could feel the blood pulsating at his temples, his head pounding with frenetic tension, as he moved swiftly up the cobblestone path to St. Mary's Cathedral. The stifling air of the muggy night pulled at him, every muscle in his body working against it. The magnificent structure of deity towered over him and he dared not look up for fear the angry beast would crush him. As his fingertips grazed the large rustic handle of the wooden door, it began to move of its own accord, slowly at first, then riveting with a thunderous roar. With legs of lead, Adam forced himself forward through the foyer, terrified of what awaited inside. To his astonishment, Father Jacob stood at the front of the church, the altar rising up behind him like an army of armored soldiers protecting their own. The light of votive candles danced about the vast cathedral, illuminating the deathly white face and hands of the majestic looking priest.

Momentarily frightened by the intimidating sight, Adam managed to break the chains of fear that bound him to the entrance.

"Who are you?" he called out, his voice echoing off the vigilant statues that watched the confrontation from their exalted perches.

"Your confessor," the rumbling voice of Father Jacob announced.

"Then accept my confession!" Adam cried out, falling to his knees upon the cold marble floor. "Forgive me Father for I have sinned—"

"It is too late," the priest interrupted.

Adam looked into the dark face of the unyielding priest. "For what?! Too late to repent?! I am repentant Father! I can see the damage that I've done and am still doing! But I can't stop it unless you put me back into my own body!"

"I'm afraid I can't do that. Time must take its course."

"But they'll die, just like they did before," Adam countered.

"That is up to you. You now have the advantage of fore-sight," the Priest said.

Adam leaped to his feet in anger. "What is this? Some kind of chess game to you? To pit a man against himself?!"

"You came to me for forgiveness," the priest reminded.

"So give me a penance," Adam begged.

"If you truly understand your sins, you will give yourself a penance. If not, you will go on as you have in the past as Adam Claiborne with no recollection of any of this."

"What does that mean?" Adam asked in frustration. "You're speaking in riddles!"

From behind Adam the angelic sound of Monique's voice called out to him. "Adam?"

He turned to see the beautiful figure of Monique silhouetted in the door. "I can't find my baby without you," she beckoned, resembling more an apparition than reality.

Adam turned back to the altar, but Father Jacob was gone. "Father Jacob?" he cried out.

"Adam, please," Monique cried softly.

He turned back to her pleading face. He knew that once he left the church he would be on his own. He would be forced to fight against himself in the battle for her family's safety. He

196

looked back to the altar but there was still no sign of the mysterious priest.

"Father Jacob?!" he shrieked with all his might, the vast structure swallowing his appeal and spitting it back out into the emptiness.

"There's no one there," Monique pleaded, stepping into the light to take him by the arm. She was no apparition, her beauty was real and she needed him desperately. "Please, let's go," she whispered.

Chapter 28

The taxi cab stood idling, while Kyle peered through the wrought iron gate, down the long row of oak trees stretching to the Claiborne Mansion. To Kyle's relief he could see Marshal's Pontiac parked in front of the entrance, the house lit up with occupants. He had lost sight of the car when his taxicab nearly plowed into a semi. He had only been guessing that they would return with the child to his brother's home when he redirected the cabby in the direction of the estate. Kyle pulled a few bills from his pocket and paid the driver. "Thanks for the tip," the cabby sneered, then spat a wad of tobacco in the direction of Kyle's shoes.

"Hey you son-of-a-bitch," Kyle screamed, dancing to miss the hurling slime. He kicked at the fleeing taxicab, but was forced to back off when the spinning tires blasted him with hundreds of tiny pebbles.

"I'll get you later," Kyle promised in a grumble, wiping the dirt from his eyes. He punched the buzzer to the gate.

"Who is it?" Eli's voice crackled over the speaker.

"Who the hell do you think it is?" Kyle growled, facing into the video monitor. "Don't you recognize me by now you dumb shit?"

Inside the security room, Eli looked closer at the video monitor. Kyle glared through the screen, his thin muscular body and drawn face accentuated by the distorted image. Eli quickly hit the gate release button, and apologized through the speaker. Although Kyle was much smaller than himself, he carried a bigger bite. Like the rest of the Claiborne household, Eli avoided him, taking extreme caution to stay out of his sometimes explosive path.

The gate opened with a whine and Kyle passed through on his way up the long drive to the mansion. "Okay . . . okay . . . think, you idiot, think," he said aloud still trying to concoct a story for his brother. His heart began to race as the huge oaks gathered behind him, the light of the mansion drawing near. Still his mind drew a blank. He fumbled through his pocket for the coke vial and for a brief moment of agony, thought he had lost it in the shuffle with Sinclair. Finally, his fingers located the tiny container and pulled it from his pocket. He hesitated at the foot of the long, wooden porch and opened the container. Muffled conversation seeped through the open windows to the outside. He strained to hear what the voices were saying, but the thick shrubbery was filled with the shrill reverberation of crickets and belching bullfrogs. To his dismay, their noisy presence denied him the insight as to what sort of mood awaited him behind the walls. The front door quietly unlatched and floated open, revealing Soley in his usual dark suit.

"Good evening, sir," he greeted.

Kyle was irritated by the sight of the thin butler. "Soulman, you got a bad habit of lurking around all the time," he heckled. In spite of Soley's presence, Kyle put the vial to his nostril and took a hit of confidence in preparation for facing his brother. The servant watched with neither disapproval nor surprise upon his elderly face.

* * * * *

"What the hell is he doing?" Claiborne called out from within, then went to the doorway. The moment he saw Kyle standing at the foot of the porch, in the light of the open door, he could tell by his brother's disheveled appearance and slightly frenzied eyes that he was wired. "You look like shit," he fumed.

"Gee thanks for your observation . . . boss," Kyle said with his ever-present smile in the face of hostility. He had learned at an early age that the one protection he had against his brother was his smile. No matter what attacks his older opponent would hurl, the smile acted as a shield against exposing his underbelly. Nothing irked his brother more than the act of insolence.

Claiborne stepped back into the foyer, fully expecting that Kyle would immediately follow. He joined his wife, Emily, who had Amy on her lap, tugging away at the child's fine golden hair with a brush. Marshal was slouched on a chair in the corner of the room in his usual slumber. Claiborne had already sent his son, Philip, to his room for the evening. He didn't want the boy exposed to the gruesome details of his work.

After a few minutes, Kyle sauntered into the bright room.

"All right," Claiborne said, pacing back and forth, "what the hell was that all about in the Quarter?"

Kyle took a sigh, put his voice on auto pilot and went along for the ride. "Well, you're not going to be happy to hear this, but they refused to hand over the fifty-two thousand."

"Excuse me . . . did . . . you've . . . they what?!" Claiborne stammered.

"They wouldn't give me the money, and when I checked, they didn't have it on 'em," he explained.

"What the hell did they do with it?" Claiborne demanded.

"They said they hid it somewhere along the way, but wouldn't tell me where. I was about to beat it out of 'em when the cops drove past," he said.

"You let them leave without handing over fifty-two thousand of my money?" Claiborne demanded.

The lie, taking shape and becoming reality, convinced its creator he had the right to stand up for himself. "What the hell else was I supposed to do?" Kyle yelled back. "You saw the cops."

Claiborne looked around at the child in dismay. "What about her? They're just going to leave her?"

"I guess they figured the money was more important," Kyle said.

"Oh, how disgusting," Emily gasped.

Claiborne walked to the open window, trying to control his mounting anger. He felt like a fool. He had tried to give the couple the benefit of the doubt, especially Monique, and she had betrayed him.

Kyle stepped toward the silk curtains. "Including the unpaid balance on their loan, that makes you fifty-six thousand down," he emphasized.

Claiborne wheeled around on him. "Thanks to your incompetence!" he spat.

Emily abandoned the child's matted hair and climbed atop her towering heels. "Fifty-six thousand for the life of a child? I'm sure Mrs. Cleary could easily locate a fine, proper couple that would pay that amount for the baby. I can call her if you want," she offered.

Claiborne turned vaguely toward his wife. "What did you say?"

Emily gathered the child into her arms. "Never mind, I'll take care of it," she said and disappeared up the stairs.

* * * * *

The old car quietly rolled across the gravel, the clanking sound of its engine and its beaming headlights squelched fifty feet back. The moment Adam hit the brakes he regretted it; the absence of pads ground metal on metal sending a screeching noise that would alert someone a block away to their arrival. In spite of his trepidation, the high-pitched squeal went unnoticed, lost within the rhythm of the night sounds.

"This is where you live?" Monique asked in awe of the immense estate that sprawled out behind the gate.

"Yes," Adam answered.

Monique was silent as if taking it all in.

"If they catch us out here," Adam said, "they'll send Marshal off with Amy to lure us away from the house."

Monique became alarmed at the dreadful thought. "What do you mean?"

"Don't worry, we're not going to let them know we're here until we're inside where I can tell our side of the story. No matter what, though, if you see Marshal leaving with Amy, don't follow. We'll catch up to him later," he explained.

"Where would he take her?" she asked.

He didn't want to answer. "Look, let's just get inside without being caught. You see that camera over there?" he asked pointing to a monitor above the gate.

202

"Yeah."

"Well, there's several of those scattered about, but my security guard is an idiot and he'll probably have one of the monitors on 'I Love Lucy'. It shouldn't be too hard to sneak past. Come on," he said, reaching for the door.

The couple carefully got out of the car, opting to leave their doors open rather than fight the sound of shutting them. Monique touched the cool iron of the gate, peering through to the intimidating sight of the huge mansion. Adam recognized the fear she held behind her set jaw and determined eyes.

"As soon as we're over, we'll run like hell to that side of the house," he said, pointing to a row of bushes close to the front of the mansion.

Monique made an impressively quick climb up the swayed oak and a fearless drop over the tall security fence. Adam immediately followed, slightly embarrassed that he was not nearly as adept at climbing as she. He dropped to the other side with a thud and a sharp pain in his arthritic shoulder.

"Are you okay?" Monique asked.

"Yeah," he muttered, then got to his feet. He slowly reached down and took her warm soft hand into his own. He held it gently, yet with strength, as if to reassure her that he would be there for her. She stared back at him, taken by the moment.

"Let's go," he said quietly, then led her out across the lawn where they ran past the looming oaks to the cover of the shrubbery. Once they were under the safety of the bushes, they fell against the soft ground breathing heavily. From where they lay, they could see through the window of the security room, where Eli's face glowed under the blue lights of the many monitors. He was busy chewing on a ham sandwich, engrossed in a game of "Wheel of Fortune".

"I never thought I'd be breaking into my own house, spying

on my own incompetent guard," Adam whispered, wiping the sweat from his eyes.

"Okay, see that side door?" he asked, pointing to an entrance connected to the kitchen. "That's almost always left open by the maid. I'll check it, then wave you on if it's clear," he instructed before starting out across the final stretch of the lawn.

* * * * *

Amy sat with her small head leaning against the mahogany leg of Emily's desk inside the master bedroom. Her eyes were heavy, as she fought to keep back the blanket of slumber.

"You're going to love her," Emily raved, seated at the desk with a telephone receiver in hand. She was making great points with Mrs. Cleary. Even though it was very late, the old woman had been very receptive to her call. "She's adorably pretty with beautiful big eyes," she continued, wondering if Mrs. Cleary would repay the favor by getting her into the Joshua Club. She had wanted to join for years but only the wealthiest, most elite were allowed in and it took considerable campaigning even then. Although Emily had known the Clearys all her life—she had been a childhood friend of their daughter's—she had never felt comfortable in asking for the favor. Now, she would certainly be able to. She listened attentively as the receiver talked back to her, carrying the golden approval of Mrs. Cleary.

"Why certainly, Emily," the old woman's voice crowed. "If she's as pretty as you say, Jake will have no problem placing her."

Jake Cleary, a wealthy attorney, had gone into the business of black marketing babies as a service to society. He felt that if parents couldn't give their children a decent home, why not sell them to someone who could? The parents would be relieved of the burden of rearing children they didn't want and couldn't afford, while couples who wanted children could have them without suffering the pompous scrutiny of adoption agencies. "I'm sort of a modern-day Robin Hood," the old man would snort proudly, but ever so discreetly, to his friends. "Without my help the children would grow up in poverty. With my help, they get the wealthiest of family inheritances plopped into their tiny laps." He never flaunted his prosperous business too openly though, for fear he would end up behind bars.

Emily got up from her chair, her own excitement too much to contain seated. Everything was working out splendidly for all involved. Her husband would get his money back . . . the child would have a better home . . . the Clearys would make a tidy little profit . . . and she could finally press Mrs. Cleary for the membership. As Emily walked about the room, smiling with contentment, she passed by the lofty windows, and nearly dropped the receiver when a movement from outside caught her eyes. She peered out into the dark yard, spotting someone hunched alongside the bushes. Although she was momentarily frightened by the figure, her fright was soon replaced by panic when she realized that it was probably one of the parents of the child she was claiming for Mrs. Cleary.

"Listen, Mrs. Cleary," she said as calmly as she could into the telephone, "I'll have to get back to you in a few minutes. The little darling needs a bottle."

She snatched the sleeping child from the floor and raced down the long winding staircase to the living room where her husband and Kyle were in the midst of a heated argument.

"You've got to kill them!" Kyle insisted, his voice rising above his brother's. "If the word gets around that—"

205

"Don't tell me how to run my business," Claiborne hissed. "And keep your damn voice down. I've got a kid upstairs who doesn't need to hear this kind of shit!"

"Adam!" Emily wailed. "There's someone on the property."

The two men turned to her, their argument reaching a jolting halt.

"God damn it," Claiborne said heatedly under his breath. "I told that son-of-a-bitch never to come here again!" He turned to Marshal who had been roused earlier from his nap by the loud commotion. "Get Eli on the phone and tell him to bring them inside," he commanded.

Upon hearing the order, Marshal looked at Kyle as if he were going to lose his dinner. "Okay," he said, with feigned enthusiasm, hoping his partner would come to the rescue.

"You can't do that," Kyle said, turning toward his brother. "What if they have a gun or something? Or what if that cop car followed them from the Quarter? You've got to get them away from here," he urged.

Claiborne pulled a pack of antacids from his pocket and popped a couple in his mouth while everyone stood by breathlessly awaiting his response. Finally, Kyle couldn't take the suspense any longer and decided to take matters into his own hands. "I'll get rid of them," he offered, heading for the door.

"Hold on a God-damned second, I don't want you to take care of anything," Claiborne called out. "We need to deal with this away from the house."

"What about her?" Emily asked, referring to the little toddler who stood beside her. Claiborne looked down at Amy who had been forgotten in the debate.

"They would find a good home for her," Emily suggested, thrusting a piece of paper into her husband's hand. "Not only would they give her good parents, but they're willing to pay you the fifty-six thousand you've lost."

Claiborne looked at the Cleary's name and address written across the fine paper in his wife's flamboyant writing. Cleary was a highly respected name and they would probably find the child a better life than she would have with the Sinclairs. Besides, hadn't the Sinclairs in essence already sold their child by abandoning her for the money? A parent willing to compromise their child for any amount of money wasn't fit to be a parent. Yes, the child would be better off with a couple who really wanted her. "Marshal, copy this down," Claiborne ordered, handing the paper to him.

Emily was quick to offer a pen and piece of paper. While Marshal scribbled down the name and address, Claiborne gave the instructions.

"Take the child to the Clearys at that address, but don't go straight there. I want you to make sure the Sinclairs see you leaving. Once you see they're following, go out through Jasper Woods on the south side of the Westbank. Keep going until you know that Kyle and I have caught up to them, then take the baby on to the Clearys," he ordered.

Emily handed the sleepy toddler to Marshal. "I'll call and tell her you're on your way. She insisted on paying with cash so I'll tell her to have it ready."

Claiborne looked warningly at Marshal. "Don't screw it up," he advised the fidgety man who avoided his stare by looking over at Kyle. Claiborne followed his line of sight to his brother, catching a glimpse of the two men's uneasiness.

"What?" Kyle asked, feeling as if he were being scrutinized.

"Did I say something to you?" Claiborne asked, sensing an air of secrecy between Kyle and Marshal.

Kyle didn't answer, only stared at his brother with a thumping heart.

"Get going," Claiborne finally ordered, breaking the silence. With sweaty palms, Marshal handed back the original piece of paper with the address and Claiborne stuffed it into his suit jacket.

* * * * *

Adam approached the side of the mansion with extreme caution. Light shone out the window panes of the kitchen door, forcing him to step from the darkness in order to check if it was unlocked. He peered inside the empty kitchen as he clicked the handle, which gave way. He breathed a sigh of relief and motioned back to Monique who waited in the shadows.

Monique saw his signal and ran out toward him, leaving the cover of the bushes. Suddenly, she heard the grinding clatter of a starting engine coming from the front drive; she froze in the middle of the lawn, her heart beating frantically. She remembered what Adam had said about Marshal taking her baby and wondered if maybe they had already been caught and he was stealing away with her child that very minute.

"Monique," Adam whispered from the door, "come on."

But Monique couldn't resist; she had to see if her worry was founded. She sprinted to the front of the mansion and to her abhorrence saw the Pontiac, with Marshal behind the wheel, rolling slowly down the gravel drive toward the gate. Panic overtook her when she spotted Amy standing in the seat beside him.

"No! You bastard!" she screamed, running into the drive after him.

Adam quickly rounded the corner of the mansion to see Monique chasing after the creeping vehicle.

Monique fumbled for the passenger handle and when she finally got a grip on it, found it was locked. From inside, Amy saw her mother and burst into tears. The sight of the crying toddler with her outstretched arms wrenched Monique's heart.

"It's okay, baby," she called out to the screaming child as she ran alongside the moving car. "Mama's here." She pressed her hands against the glass. "Please," she begged, but Marshal met her desperation with a grotesque sneer. She pounded her fists against the window. "Let me in!" she cried.

Monique felt a sense of relief when Marshal's hand went to the power window switch, but instead of opening the passenger window, as she expected, he opened his own. He tossed the canister of Proventil out, then pressed his foot on the gas pedal. She screamed out in agony as the car sped from her reach, leaving the Proventil clinking in the rocks behind it. She retrieved the medicine from the ground, just as the security gate parted and released the Pontiac from the estate.

"No," she cried and ran for her car.

"Monique, wait!" Adam called out to her. "You're falling into a trap!"

His voice went unheeded as she slammed the doors shut to the old car and started the engine.

"They want you to follow him," Adam warned, dashing toward the passenger window.

She looked at him wildly from behind the wheel. "Where's he taking her?"

"I don't remember the address, but it's written down on a piece of paper in my suit pocket," he explained.

"Then I have to follow," she said, putting the car into gear.

"Give me a chance to get into the house to get it," he urged.

"I can't! He threw this out the window," she cried, holding up the canister of Proventil.

The puzzle to Amy's death finally fell into place for Adam, the discarded medicine the linking piece. "Oh Jesus," he heard himself say. "What have I done?"

Monique's foot bore down on the accelerator, the back wheels of the old car spitting rocks and gravel as it fish tailed to reach the solid pavement of the street. Adam leapt after her, grasping for the passenger door. "Wait! I'll go with you!"

The car ground to a halt, long enough for him to get inside before it roared forward again in pursuit.

The moment Adam shut his door, he felt like jumping back out. "I can't believe I'm going along with this," he said, shaking his head and wiping his brow.

"You don't understand, do you?" Monique asked. "Without that medicine, she could die."

"I know that," Adam replied, struggling to keep his tone calm. "I'm just trying to . . . God I don't know. I just know that . . . God damn it!" he yelled, slamming his fist against the dash. "Everything I'm doing is wrong. I'm going along with you even when I know it's wrong. I know how this ends!"

Monique thrust her foot on the brakes and Adam flew forward. "Do you want out?" she asked him, anger flashing in her eyes, the only sound was that of the idling engine.

"No," he said quietly.

"Good," she said, her face softening. She accelerated once again and the old car leapt forward and rapidly regained its speed down St. Charles Avenue.

The car bounced violently over the swells of the passing intersections, Marshal's taillights always within sight. Although Monique's car was solid steel and without all the hi-tech equipment that the newer cars afforded, its huge engine was unmatched in power and had little trouble keeping up with Marshal's Pontiac. As Monique maneuvered the car through the sparse, late night traffic, she gripped the wheel so tightly that her knuckles were white.

Adam kept watch through the back window and after a few blocks, the headlights of his own car, the Lincoln Continental, appeared behind them.

"Right on schedule," he groaned, turning forward in his seat.

"Where are we going?" Monique asked, laying on her horn to warn a Volkswagen full of teenagers that was about to roll through a stop sign.

"To the Expressway. We're headed for the swamp," he said.

She glanced at him, clearly not expecting his response. "Oh," she sighed.

"We can still get away, though. This time, we'll keep following Marshal instead of stopping at the old house that you and your husband did."

"What house?" Monique questioned.

"For some reason you stopped out on Old Shell. You deserted your car in the middle of the road and took out through the swamp until you got to the house. That's where you were killed."

"But I don't know of any house out there," Monique said.

"Look, if we don't stop, we won't have to worry about it," he calculated, hoping that would be the wrench in the cog of their destruction.

Monique kept her eyes fixed on Marshal's tail-lights, not daring to look away for even a split second. Suddenly, flashing sparks shot out from beneath his tires, as the Pontiac screeched to miss a pick-up truck that cut across its path.

"Oh my God," Monique cried out, watching helplessly from behind as her daughter's life was put into jeopardy.

"She'll be okay," Adam reassured her, just as the Pontiac made it past without a scratch.

"That son-of-a-bitch is going to kill her," she cried.

"No he won't, she makes it to the Clearys fine," Adam said before he could catch himself. He hadn't planned on telling her the gruesome details of where Marshal was headed.

Monique looked toward him. "What do you mean the Clearys? Who are the Clearys?" she asked.

Adam looked away from her questioning eyes to the houses and shops that sped past. "They . . . they deal in illegal adoption."

Monique looked toward him. "What?" she asked weakly.

"They were willing to reimburse me for the money I thought you'd stolen in exchange for Amy," he explained, refusing to look at her.

"Oh God," Monique whispered.

"When I thought you'd chosen the money over her," he said. "I . . . uh . . . I don't know what I was thinking," he said with a heavy sigh.

Monique stared ahead, her shoulders pinched with worry. "Do they know she's sick?"

"No," he answered. "I didn't know, and I doubt that Marshal would tell them."

Chapter 29

The night became brighter as the three speeding cars rose over the Crescent City Connection toward the West Bank, the dense city lights sparkling in the distance, across from the Mississippi River.

Monique removed one hand at a time from the wheel and stretched it out, her joints aching from clenching the wheel so tightly. Except for the churning engine and the night air, whistling through every tiny crack in the body of the car, there was a deafening silence filled with anticipation. The moon dangled in front of them like a huge yellow wafer beckoning them toward the darkened swampland. The blue highway passed beneath the tires in a hypnotic fashion, the rushing cement lulling them into a false sense of ease.

Adam pulled his stare from the window and looked back to the car behind them. He could see the silhouette of himself in the passenger seat with Kyle behind the wheel. He remembered that he had agreed to let Kyle drive his car because his nerves were shot from the stressful day.

"What do you see back there?" Monique asked.

"Nothing," he said, turning forward again.

Monique looked over at him a moment. She had never seen Charlie's face look so hard and sad. She still couldn't believe how much a person's soul could change their appearance.

The man behind Charlie's face was tired and had seen so much more than her husband had ever experienced. "I don't blame you, anymore," she said.

The face turned toward her. "You should," he said.

"But Kyle was lying to you, you didn't know all the facts."

"I knew enough."

"But you're helping me now. If you were such an evil person, you wouldn't be," she argued.

"I'm helping you because I . . . you've become my family, not because I'm a good person," he said. "I've killed others . . . you weren't my first. And put in the same situation, who's to say that I wouldn't kill your husband again, even though I know he's probably a decent person."

"I don't believe that," Monique said.

"Whatever you do, don't start believing bad people are good just because they do something decent to help themselves," he said, then turned back to the fleeting highway that floated past his window. His body felt weak and a bitter, aching feeling chewed at his stomach. He thought of his son, Philip, sleeping inside his room with no idea of what his father did for a living. He wondered what the future would hold for the timid boy. A glimmer of hope touched his thoughts. Perhaps he could change the future for his son and make it better. Hadn't the priest said that he would return to his body if he came up with a penance? So his penance to himself would be to change things and make them better. But the Sinclairs? What would happen to them? A sharp pain cut through his stomach. "Oh Jesus," he muttered. He turned his attention back to the road ahead, deciding that he needed to concentrate on the present. First he had to make sure that the couple survived along with their baby, then he would think about the future.

* * * * *

Suddenly, Marshal's car took an abrupt turn off the highway onto a dirt road.

"Ahhh!" Monique screamed, twisting the wheel and hitting the brake, sending them into a half-spin that whipped to the left and then to the right. She managed to make the turn but the back wheels went off the road and momentarily lodged behind a fallen log laying roadside. The wheels tugged with a scraping groan, then a couple of thumps, as they went up over the wood.

"How about a warning next time?" Monique requested.

"Sorry."

The dust before them began kicking up so thickly that it was hard to see the tail-lights ahead of them.

"I'm losing him," she said.

"He's there, you just can't see him," Adam said reassuringly.

The faint glow of the red lights moved in and out of the dirty cloud, as Monique strained with all her might to keep it within sight.

The whine of the old car's engine was suddenly replaced with sputtering and knocking.

"Oh no," Monique gasped, pumping her foot onto the gas pedal.

"What is it?" Adam asked.

"We're out of gas," she cried, as the engine completely died. "Oh God, we're out of gas!" she screamed, futilely pumping the pedal.

Adam read the gauge, the red lever only halfway down. "You've got half a tank!"

"It always reads half full! It's broken!"

215

The old car coasted slower and slower, Monique and Adam trapped helplessly by its surrender.

"Hit the brake," Adam ordered.

Monique jammed the brakes, bringing the car to a halt.

"Now we know why you stopped," Adam said, turning around to see how far back the Lincoln was, but the dust obstructed his view. "Come on," he said, reaching for the door.

* * * * *

The couple flew from the lighted car, and headed for the black swamp. The headlights of the Lincoln dimly appeared through the dust, as they stepped off of the dry gravel road onto the marshy ground. Their feet sank slightly into the damp bayou soil, which was perpetually sodden even in dry weather. As the mud invaded his holed shoes, Adam realized that he had forgotten about the tracks that led Kyle and himself to the Sinclairs. "Oh no," he exclaimed looking back at their steps. He grabbed a stick and quickly started etching away at the ground, trying desperately to erase their tracks.

"Come on," Monique exclaimed. "If we wait any longer, they won't need tracks to find us!"

Intense shafts of light cut through the dust, as the ever approaching Lincoln drew nearer. Adam discarded the stick and took her by the hand. They descended into the dense swamp, past tupelo gums, water oaks and bald cypress. The high-pitched squeal of their car buzzer became more and more faint, as it was gradually replaced with the eerie calls of the wild. In the distance they heard flying gravel spraying against the old car's side, as the brakes of the Lincoln burned to stop the two cars from

216

colliding. The couple paused for a moment to look back through the trees, which swallowed them up so completely it was as if they were hidden in a crowd of ominous giants. Feeling the need to see their enemies in order to gauge their advantage, they anxiously peered through the dark columns. They caught glimpses of the two brothers as their broken silhouettes moved before the headlights of the old Ford.

"Let's go," Adam urged, and they took out once again into the darkness.

They ran in silence, terror and exhaustion quickly taking their breath. Hanging limbs and slicing underbrush cut into their skin, as they dodged the seemingly alive vegetation which jumped out before them, threatening to overtake them if they hesitated too long in one spot. They stumbled blindly through the dark blanket of the marsh toward a clearing that was lit by the bright moon. Almost out of nowhere, the dilapidated white house appeared before them, perched upon the bizarre uprising in the soil. Monique fell back, terrified by the ominous sight of the house's foretold presence. "That's it, isn't it?" she gasped under her breath, feeling like a victim viewing its grave before being shoved over the side.

"Yes," Adam confirmed. "Follow me, I know where we can hide."

He rapidly ascended the slight incline with Monique reluctantly at his heels. He led her behind the house, past the fallen boards shed by the aged structure, to the cellar. He pulled open the creaky lid, exposing the stone pit just as he remembered it. Monique looked into the bizarre creation, never having seen a cellar before.

"Climb down," Adam said, pointing to the rickety wooden ladder that led past the hanging whiskey jugs into the seemingly endless abyss.

"But we'll be trapped here," she protested.

"They don't find it until after they go into the house," he reassured her.

Monique lowered her legs into the hole, and positioned her feet upon the wooden ladder. She carefully stepped downward into the black pit, while maintaining a tight grip in case her footing gave way. She reached the last step and looked wearily down at the water, hesitating to let herself fall, not knowing how deep it was or if it was infested with water moccasins.

"It's okay," Adam said, his voice echoing around her.

Monique stepped from the ladder, expecting to be instantly submerged in water, but was much relieved when it stopped at her ankles.

Adam pulled the heavy lid shut from the inside, plunging them into total darkness. After a few seconds, their eyes adjusted to the rays of moonlight that streaked through the wooden slats of the lid.

"What now?" Monique asked, rearranging a hanging jug that was jabbing into her back.

"In a few minutes, they'll be walking past to enter through the back door," he said quietly.

The coolness of the sunken shelter sent Monique's body into uncontrollable shivers. Only moments earlier, she had been drenched in sweat, and now she shook like a small child. "Oh God," she murmured and Adam put his arms around her to comfort her. "This is a nightmare," she whispered. "I'm not normally so . . . so helpless . . . it's just that when it comes to my baby," she hesitated. "What's going to happen to Amy? Please tell me."

Adam paused, trying to find the words.

218

"She dies, doesn't she?" Monique asked.

"Not if we get there in time," he said. He felt Monique's body sway against his. "Even if we make it out of here, how will we know where to look?" she asked. Although she kept her head down, Adam could tell that she was weeping.

"I promise I'll get the address from my suit jacket and the keys to the Lincoln. It's the only way," he said, tenderly lifting her eyes to him and brushing away the silent tears.

"It's hard to believe that you're the same person who's trying to kill us right now," she whispered.

"Maybe I'm not," Adam murmured taking her tightly into his grasp and gently kissing her forehead. Monique turned her sad eyes toward him and kissed him softly on the lips. They stood in silence, Adam's reassuring embrace calming her trembling body. Within moments, the silent couple heard the crunching sound of footsteps stealing past the unseen cellar. Through the slatted lid, they saw the figures of Claiborne and Kyle cautiously approaching the rear of the house, with guns poised to fire. As Adam watched himself, only twenty feet away, reenacting what seemed to him to be the past, a strange feeling overcame him. Even though he remembered so clearly the thoughts that had gone through his mind as he turned the rusty knob to the back door, he felt so removed from himself. It was if he were watching a stranger. Was the man before him having the same thought of how long it had been since the door had been opened, moving through the events just as he had before? But the events had now changed, he thought with elation. He had finally succeeded in doing something different, therefore possibly affecting the outcome. Whether or not it would work was yet to be seen.

* * * * *

219

Claiborne and Kyle quietly searched the dingy, small kitchen of the cabin before moving on to the main room. Light struggled through the opaque window casting a blue glow over their faces as they looked about the musty room. They scanned it with precision and expertise, finding no sign of their quarry. A potbelly stove obscured their sight from a darkened corner, so Claiborne motioned to Kyle. "Check behind that stove," he muttered with a wave of his gun.

Kyle crept to the corner with his pistol cocked, but discovered no one. "It's clear," he said and when he turned back to his brother, he noticed a ladder behind him, leading up to an attic door.

He caught his brother's eyes and motioned above them. Claiborne nodded him on.

Kyle's ascent up the ladder was quick; his eagerness to annihilate the couple erased all fears of confrontation. He pressed against the door, slid it open and disappeared through the opening.

Claiborne waited below, his eyes glued to the creaking boards overhead. He watched intently, catching glimpses of his brother through the spaced boards, moving about. As the boards swayed with Kyle's weight, small particles floated downward, some of them lodging painfully in Claiborne's upturned eyes.

"They're not up here," Kyle called out, the boards beginning to squeal in protest to his heavy footsteps. After a sudden brittle snapping of wood, there was a stricken silence, before a crashing thunder. Claiborne leapt for cover as the ceiling overhead opened up its belly and spewed out Kyle's flailing body.

"Ahhh!!" he screamed, as he plummeted to the hard floor already covered in splintered boards and fallen debris. As he landed with tremendous impact upon the hard floor, the sound of a snapping bone cut through the loud rumbling. Wood particles continued to fall as Kyle grabbed his leg screaming out in pain.

Claiborne quickly rummaged through the rubble to his brother's aid.

"Oh Jesus . . . oh Jesus," Kyle whimpered, his whole body shaking badly beneath the boards. "Son-of-a-bitch!" he shrieked in agony when Claiborne pulled back the pieces of wood, exposing Kyle's bloodied leg. Before Kyle could see the damage himself, Claiborne grabbed him beneath the arms and started dragging him toward a wall.

"Oh God!" Kyle cried, grabbing for his leg. "What the hell are you doing?"

"You want to get your head blown off by Sinclair?" Claiborne asked. He leaned him against the wall and raced back to find his pistol that had been buried in the mess.

* * * * *

Inside the dark cellar, Adam and Monique listened intently to decipher what was going on in the house. When they heard the crashing noise they both looked up. "What was that?" Adam asked moving toward the ladder.

"It sounded like the place is caving in," Monique whispered.

Adam slowly lifted the door to the cellar and peered out toward the house, but from his ground-level perspective he couldn't see what was happening inside. He pushed the heavy door the rest of the way open and it dropped to the ground. Moonlight rushed in upon them.

"What are you doing?" Monique asked.

"I'm just going to see what happened," he whispered back.

He pulled himself out of the pit and started to shut the door again but saw that Monique was right behind him.

"Wait here," he said.

"I'm coming with you," she asserted.

"No."

"Remember, that's my husband's body you're gambling with," she argued back.

Adam knew he had been beaten and put his hand out to make her climb quicker.

* * * * *

"Oh . . . Jesus," Kyle muttered, sweat draining down his face as he clutched his leg tightly.

"It's broken, but you'll live," Claiborne scolded quietly. "Here, take this," he urged, shoving his gun back into his belly.

Kyle reluctantly removed his hands from the blood-soaked pant leg to take the gun; as he did, his fingers scraped across a broken bone that was protruding through the material. At the sight of the bloody mutilation, he fell to the side and heaved. Claiborne stepped back to avoid the spewing vomit. Kyle rolled back over, his face extremely pale. "Oh God . . . I need something," he moaned, his shaking hands searching through his pockets. With every movement he flinched in misery.

"I'm going to go check outside, around the house," informed Claiborne.

"No! Don't leave me," Kyle pleaded, his trembling fingers

struggling with a pill bottle.

"You'll be fine, you got the gun," his brother said.

Kyle stuffed a couple of pills into his mouth and swallowed them down. "I'll be a sitting duck," he whined.

"You've got the gun," Claiborne argued.

* * * * *

Adam peeked through the crack between the kitchen door and the wall into the darkened room where Claiborne and Kyle were crouched on the floor. Upon seeing the hole in the ceiling he realized that Kyle had fallen through the exact spot where he had yanked Monique through. After a moment of surveying the two men, Adam finally got up the nerve to call out to them.

"Don't shoot and we won't either," he declared, even though his only source of defense was a board he gripped tightly between his hands.

He could see the stunned faces of the two men as they both pulled back their triggers and looked anxiously toward the kitchen. "He's bluffing," Kyle whispered. "He doesn't have a gun. I can keep you covered while you charge him," he urged quietly to Claiborne, but Claiborne wanted to hear what his opponent had to say.

"All we want is the address of the baby and the keys to your car and nobody will have to get hurt," Adam called out.

Kyle let out a snort of laughter. "You took fifty-six thousand of my brother's money and now you want his wheels! Now that's balls," he roared as his hands reached for his coke vial.

"You got a lot of nerve, buddy," Claiborne said crossly. "What happened to my money?"

223

"Why don't you ask your brother? He's the one that's been ripping you off," Adam called out.

"What do you mean?" Claiborne asked, glancing over at Kyle.

"For starters, we paid five thousand, not one," Adam said.

"You're a lying sack of shit," Kyle said uneasily before haphazardly firing a shot in the direction of the kitchen.

Adam felt the bullet whine past his cheek before lodging in the wall behind them.

"No more shots!" he called out. "I can take you both out from here."

Upon hearing his warning, the two men looked about for cover, but every part of the room was visible from the kitchen. Kyle lifted his gun once again to fire but Claiborne pulled it back down.

"Ask him about the rest of the money," Kyle insisted, his voice now shaky and broken as he went on the defensive. "What about the rest of the money you thieving bastard?"

"You already made the rounds, Kyle, and you damn well know it!" Adam said vehemently.

"That's bullshit," Kyle quipped. "My brother's not stupid enough to believe that, he saw you make the rounds himself!"

"You kidnaped this woman's baby! We had no other choice," Adam called out. "We were just stool pigeons!"

Claiborne looked suspiciously down at Kyle.

Kyle met his stare, his own eyes becoming increasingly panicked, sweat drenching his pale skin. A smile came across his face. "Oh Jesus," he said, "you don't believe that crap do you?"

Kyle saw the doubt in his brother's eyes. "Oh come on! He's full of shit! Ask Marshal!" he wailed.

Anger shot through Adam, at the sight of his squirming brother. "That stupid ox will say whatever you tell him to say!"

224

The more Kyle fidgeted, the more guilty he appeared. Claiborne's mind began to race, Adam's words plucking away at the already fragile trust between him and his wayward brother.

"Here, check my wallet," Kyle offered, pulling it painfully from his pants. "Aahh!" he screamed. "I don't believe this," he whimpered as he pathetically held out the wallet for inspection.

"You won't find it there because he already blew it up his nose," Adam cursed.

"Why don't you just shut the hell up?" Kyle yelled.

"He already spent your money," Adam continued relentlessly, needling away. "He collected from everyone on the ledger over a month ago and now that there's no one else to get money from, he's going out on his own." Adam's anger was building along with Claiborne's suspicion. "The last name on the list was a new client. Ask him who was at that address!"

Claiborne stared down at Kyle. "Who was it?" he demanded. "The only people I've lent to in that building were the Sinclairs."

"I don't know what he's talking about," Kyle sobbed, again feeling the pain of the break. He uncapped the coke vial and started to put it to his nose, but Claiborne snatched it from his hands.

"Who was it?" his brother demanded, the sight of the ever-present white powder sending a surge of anger through him.

"Oh Christ," Kyle cried, "I can't believe you're going to take their side . . . I mean Jesus . . . Adam . . . we're brothers . . . oh God," he groped for the bottle of pills that he had replaced in his pocket and dumped some of them into his mouth. "I can't take this pain . . . I can't."

Claiborne slapped the pills from his hand, scattering them across the floor. "If you're not going out on your own, who was the last collection?" he asked through clenched teeth. "Tell me!"

"It was no one," Kyle said, reaching for the tiny red pills. He looked weak and thin, worn down by too many years of drugs and alcohol.

At the pathetic sight of his floundering brother, whose filthy hands groped fervently for the pills, Claiborne's heart filled with anguish. Suddenly, he grabbed Kyle's hands to stop him and when Kyle looked feverishly up at him, Claiborne slapped him across the face. "You son-of-a-bitch!" he bellowed. "What kind of mess have you gotten me into?" he demanded, pulling Kyle forward by his shirt. No longer able to take the despicable sight of his brother's wasted life, his hands went down upon the pallid face. "Tell me!" he cried, slapping him again. "You son-of-a-bitch . . . you son-of-a-bitch . . . Why can't you just stop?! . . . Why can't you just STOP?!"

Kyle's head flew back and knocked against the wall, his eyes glassy and his face beet red. Claiborne suddenly stopped and looked down at his crying brother, who folded up weeping like a child. After a few seconds, he stood to his feet and looked about the room, momentarily losing sight of the danger. "Oh God, I don't know . . . I don't," and he moved weakly toward the window, trying to regain his composure.

With the cocaine and amphetamines scalding through his veins, Kyle's whimpering quickly turned to acidic anger, while the tears continued to fall. His face twisted with anguished pain as he glowered up at Claiborne. His trembling hand fidgeted with the gun at his side, his vision blurring in and out of focus. The anger mounted into rage as his mind sped through the years and years of humiliation and torment inflicted upon him by his relentless brother. His clouded sight rested upon the back of Claiborne's neck, his eyes zeroing in on the target. His finger touched the trigger and began to squeeze.

Through the crack, Adam saw the gun rise up and after a

226

stunned moment of disbelief, he realized that he was about to witness his own murder at the hands of his wasted brother. Adrenaline took hold, thrusting him forward with the board in hand. He swung with all his might, and just as the board met the steel of the pistol a bullet exploded from its chamber and ricocheted off the ceiling and walls. Claiborne swung around with pistol drawn, to witness what appeared to be an attack on Kyle. Adam dropped the board and scrambled to retrieve Kyle's gun. Kyle, rapidly sinking into delirium, weakly grabbed at Adam's leg, who in turn cold-cocked him across the face with his foot sending him over the edge of unconsciousness.

From the kitchen doorway, Monique saw Claiborne take aim at Adam, and she leapt forward to try and stop him from firing. "No!" she cried as the shot rang out.

Adam heard the shot and looked up to see Monique falling back through the kitchen, clutching her shoulder. His hands finally grasped the cool handle of Kyle's pistol and as he swung it on Claiborne, he was met with an oncoming shot.

"Get out of here Moon!" Adam screamed as he fell to the floor for cover. Claiborne fired again, as Adam crawled back into the kitchen. He saw the trail of blood leading to the back door where Monique had escaped to the outside.

"Monique, are you okay?" he called out but heard no reply. The sudden silence was deafening. He looked back toward the living room, and with the exception of the unconscious Kyle, the room appeared to be empty. Adam's stomach dropped when he saw that the front door to the cabin was standing wide open with Claiborne nowhere in sight. "Oh my God," he gasped and ran out the back door to Monique's aid.

He bolted out of the cabin into the bright moonlight. "Monique?" he called out, his voice swallowed up by the foreboding swamp. He rounded the corner of the house, spotting

227

Claiborne holding Monique at gunpoint against the wall. A shot rang out in his direction, so he fell back around the corner, edging tightly against the side of the house.

"All we want is the address," Adam called out, his words met with silence. His legs began to shake, as he realized that they were running out of time. The baby would soon be dead. "The child has acute asthma. She'll die if we don't get to her!" he cried out helplessly.

"What happened to your stutter, you slick talking bastard?" Claiborne retorted. "There's nothing wrong with that baby, I was with her all day!"

"Her attacks are sporadic," Adam argued.

"You're really smooth, aren't you? Playing me against my own brother!"

Adam edged himself closer to the corner of the house where Claiborne was holding Monique about fifteen feet on the other side; he could hear her heavy breathing and groans of pain. Adam pulled the gun to shoulder height, and suddenly rounded the corner of the house with the gun trained on Claiborne. As the face of himself came into focus, he could see the fear and the hatred directed back at him, Monique, pale and shaking in his arms.

"You won't shoot her," he said steadily, edging forward a few steps along the wall toward them, his hand trembling with the gun aimed at Claiborne. "You can't. You're in love with her," he said looking into Monique's eyes. As he looked back up to himself, a smile came across the familiar face which stared back at him.

"I already did," Claiborne said, cocking the gun leveled at her head.

"That bullet was meant for me," Adam replied, staring into the terrified eyes of the man before him. His heart ached for himself, knowing he would never be able to break through the fear in time to save the child.

"Forgive me Father for I have sinned," he whispered as he steadied his shaking hand by gripping the gun tighter. "My penance is . . . " He took a deep breath and his finger slowly started to press against the trigger. " . . . death."

Monique heard the words and horror came across her face. "Don't do it," she begged, looking beseechingly into his eyes.

Suddenly, Claiborne shoved Monique aside, and aimed his pistol at Adam, but before he could fire, a bullet blasted through his chest.

Adam, amazed that he had actually pulled the trigger, saw the dark stain of blood appearing on the suit of the man before him. As Claiborne's knees began to buckle, Adam felt dizziness and vertigo and suddenly he realized that he was the one falling to the ground wounded from the gunshot. He looked up and met the eyes of Charlie Sinclair who stood before him watching in horror, the smoking pistol in his hand.

As his body hit the soft, moist ground, a warm comforting feeling came over him, plunging him into a dreamy haze that made the stars above him dance together like fireflies. A dark figure in robes appeared above him and as the figure bent to his side, he saw that it was Father Jacob. His eyes were gentle, his voice low and fatherly.

"You were willing to sacrifice yourself so that others may live. You are now truly free from your sins, my son. I absolve you in the name of the Father, and the Son, and the Holy Ghost." His words trailed away and were soon replaced with an angelic voice whispering in the distance. A sense of overwhelming peace accompanied the voice as it touched upon his soul. The caressing sound drew nearer, and he recognized it to be Monique.

229

"Adam . . . " she said gently. He opened his eyes to see Monique withdrawing her lips from his forehead. Tears were streaming from her eyes which were filled with more love than he had ever witnessed. "You're going to be okay," she whispered with a shaky smile.

His hand lifted to his pocket, and in spite of his moist suit, he felt no pain. He removed a slip of paper and held it weakly out to her. "Kyle has the keys," he said.

"I can't leave you here like this," she cried softly.

"Go, you've got to hurry," he urged.

"I'll send . . . someone . . . " but she stopped. She could see the distant look in his eyes. "I'll never forget you," she whispered, then kissed him again, only this time, tenderly on the lips.

For the first time in his life, Adam was filled with peace. Her soft gentle kiss was the last thing he felt as his world faded to black.

Chapter 30

The first glow of morning crept through the shadows. Monique sat in silence, weakened and dazed by her injury and the task at hand.

"M-M-Moon," she heard a voice call from behind. She looked back to see Charlie, her Charlie, standing innocently alone, the gun hanging limply from his hand. "Oh Charlie!" she cried, rushing into his arms, her gunshot wound momentarily forgotten.

Charlie held her tenderly until she pulled back with anxious eyes. "You've b-b-been shot," he said, astonished by the sight of her blood-covered dress. "What . . . ?"

"We've got to go, Charlie," she explained, trying to stay calm. "Amy's in trouble!"

She quickly made her way into the old house, where Kyle lay on the floor breathing heavily with his eyes closed. As Monique bent over him to search for the keys, she saw for the first time, how much he resembled his brother, Adam. Her heart sank. The evil was gone from his face, replaced with the look of a small boy. She quickly pulled at all of his pockets and was horrified to find the keys missing. She looked back to the huge pile of rubble and knew there would be no time to dig through all of it. "Charlie?" she called out. "Can you still hot wire a car?"

* * * * *

Although exhausted from having pulled a thirty-six-hour shift, Detective Briggs moseyed along the dirt road feeling quite content, scratching at a couple of fresh mosquito bites he had gotten in the woods only a few minutes earlier. He smiled down at his newly retrieved watch thinking how lucky he was to have spotted it hanging from the low lying branch where it had been so ruthlessly snagged from his wrist. As his eyes lifted back to the road, the bumper of the old Ford was suddenly upon him, stopped squarely in the path ahead of him. "Holy shit!" he exclaimed and hit the brakes.

The undercover car skidded within inches of the Ford, stopping just before impact. Briggs sat back a moment, breathing a sigh of relief, staring at the stalled car ahead of him. "What the hell?" he muttered to himself as he slowly opened his door to investigate the situation.

A small dust cloud, created by his skidding tires, hovered around the Ford, obscuring the Lincoln parked in front of it. Upon closer inspection of the beat up old car, he recognized it to be the one that a young woman had pulled up in the day before, to pick up the pulverized Sinclair. As the dust settled, he realized that there was another vehicle parked ahead. He approached slowly, noting that the tag was Adam Claiborne's. A lump began to form in his throat as he sensed that he had stumbled upon a bad situation.

"I've almost g-got it," he heard a young man stammer from inside of the car. To Briggs's surprise, he saw the same, tattered young couple crouched in the front seat of the expensive car. The young man was attempting to hot wire it; the woman's dress was covered in blood. Briggs grabbed for his gun but found

232

only an empty holster. He instantly chastised himself for carelessly leaving his weapon lying on his front seat.

Monique looked up, just as Briggs turned to run back to his car. "Hey, we need your help!" she cried out.

As Briggs grabbed his gun from the front seat of his car, Charlie and Monique stepped out of the Lincoln and headed toward him. "Freeze!" he called out swinging the pistol at them.

"Wait, you've got this all wrong," Charlie said, stopping in his tracks.

"Put your hands up," Briggs commanded.

The couple quickly obliged, but as Monique's arms went up she winced in pain. For the first time, Briggs realized that she had been shot.

"We're just trying to get our baby," she cried. "She'll die if we don't get to her!"

Briggs looked nervously at the couple. "Where's Claiborne?" he asked.

"He's back in there about a quarter of a mile," Monique said, pointing to the swamp. "Him and his brother Kyle. He's . . . he's dead, but his brother is alive. He's hurt badly and needs an ambulance."

"Looks like you do too, lady," Briggs offered, with his gun still drawn.

"No, I need you to take me to my baby," she said and slowly opened her hand and held out the piece of paper that Adam had given her. "This is the address where she's at."

Briggs studied the weary couple, considering the situation. The young man certainly had taken a beating from the Claiborne brothers the day before and was probably justified in whatever actions he may have taken against them.

"Please, mister," Monique cried. "If we don't get there in time, she'll die!"

After a moment, Briggs lowered his gun. "Okay, get in," he said pointing to his car.

"Charlie, the kit," she said weakly. Charlie quickly leaned inside the old Ford and from the glove box, pulled out a sandwich bag with another canister of Proventil, a syringe, and a small bottle of liquid.

Monique got into the back seat of Briggs's car and lay her head on the seat. Charlie kept his eyes on her from the front while the detective radioed for an ambulance to help the Claibornes.

"I think you sh . . . sh . . . should send one to that address too, for my wife," Charlie suggested to Briggs, pointing to the address of the Clearys.

Briggs was surprised by the friendliness of Charlie's face. He had seemed so hard and cold when he had ran into him at the police station the day before. "Sure," he said.

Chapter 31

Georgette Cleary ran her sixty-nine year old finger down the obituary column in search of any familiar names. Lately, it had seemed that her old classmates were dying off in droves and she wanted to remain abreast of the situation. Although Mrs. Cleary appeared to be a very composed, intelligent woman, she was consumed with the fear of dying to the point of hysteria. She was terrified of death and was convinced that the cold hand of the grim reaper would swoop down for her soon. While most people obsessed on not getting old, Mrs. Cleary obsessed on not getting old enough. She visited her doctors regularly—at least once a week—and avoided leaving the house unnecessarily. She read the causes of death of the newly departed, speculating which of the afflictions would be the ax that severed her from life. The only problem with her delving into obituary doom for the answer was that cirrhosis of the liver wasn't listed. Each morning she sucked on a double Bloody-Mary oblivious to the fact that the future culprit was right beneath her red, shriveled nose.

When she heard the clumping of her maid coming down the stairs, her brow furrowed. It was only a matter of seconds before the flighty servant would come bounding into the dining room in a frenzy. The little bat had never learned how to deal with children, she mused.

"It's the new baby, ma'am!" the thin voice squawked behind her. "She's not breathing!"

Mrs. Cleary sighed, took a sip of her drink, then adjusted her spectacles. "Don't be incompetent, Hailey," she said, her head perched over the paper. "She probably needs to burp."

"No ma'am!" the maid argued. "She's turning blue and—"

"Don't overreact," interrupted Mrs. Cleary. "Pat her back."

Hailey fluttered between the doorway, staring at the back of her boss' beehive, struggling with the notion of one more interruption, when the doorbell suddenly rang, vibrating through the marble halls of the mansion.

Mrs. Cleary turned. "I'm not expecting anyone," she said. "See who that is."

Torn in too many directions, the maid stared back at her with dismay. "But ma'am," she finally managed to babble, "the baby!"

"Never mind, then," snapped Mrs. Cleary and she rose from her throne and marched to the door, freeing Hailey to disappear back up the stairs.

* * * * *

Although it was a bright morning, Monique felt as if she were standing in a pitch black tomb. "What if they don't answer?" she asked. It felt like an eternity since the detective had pushed the doorbell.

Finally, the heavy white door swung open, revealing a tall gray woman dressed in a suit. Her stern eyes went from the detective to Charlie and then to the bloody dress of Monique.

"Are you Georgette Cleary?" Briggs asked, holding up his

badge as identification. Before the dumbfounded woman could reply, Monique shoved past her through the door into the elegant foyer.

"Wait!" Mrs. Cleary cried. "You can't—"

With no regard for the huffing socialite, Charlie followed his wife inside.

"Amy?" the couple shouted out, racing from room to room of the lower level of the expansive home. They repeated the child's name again and again, but found the rooms to be empty. Suddenly, Hailey appeared on the upstairs landing. "Come quick, Mrs. Cleary," Hailey wailed. "I think she's dead!"

Monique looked up at the maid in horror, her words rendering her momentarily immobile. With Charlie at her side, she found the strength to move forward. They bound up the stairs in leaps, Charlie carrying the kit he had retrieved from the car.

When Monique burst through the open door into the posh nursery, her own heart stopped at the sight of Amy's lifeless blue body lying atop a diaper changing station. Monique grabbed her daughter into her arms and laid her on the floor, while Charlie pulled the needle and serum from the plastic bag and began preparing the medicine.

Monique put her lips to the nose of the tiny, celestial face, and began trying to resuscitate the toddler with her own breath. As she worked diligently, the sweet smell of Amy's tender skin and the curls wafting along her delicate forehead was more than the mother could handle.

"Hurry!" she cried out to her husband who tapped the needle to release the air bubbles. He bent over the child inserting the adrenaline into her.

"Please, God, please," Monique cried.

Finally, the weak little chest began to heave, gasping once again for life. Monique quickly grabbed the canister of Proventil and placed it to the baby's mouth, squirting a dose to help her breath. The medicine took effect almost immediately and the sound of her raspy breath became less strained, until, at last, her eyes fluttered open and she began to cry.

"Oh Amy, my baby!" Monique smiled, gathering the frightened child into her arms and holding her close. She tasted the soft wet cheeks of her crying daughter, elated by her tears. She was alive and safe, once again in her mother's arms.

Chapter 32

Monique clicked off the fluorescent light above her bed and let her hand relax to her side. She could hear the chatter and occasional laughter of the night staff as they gathered around the nurse's station just outside her door. The light, spilling in from the hallway, danced on the shiny floor beside her bed. Although the commotion would probably keep her awake, she was relieved that they had left the door open. For some reason she felt frightened of being left in the darkness.

Even though she could hear the breathing of a patient on the other side of the curtains, she felt terribly alone. She turned her eyes up to the ceiling wishing that the night were ending instead of just beginning.

She thought about Charlie. He had been so sweet and attentive. He had begged the nurses to let him stay, but they wouldn't hear of it. After the police had finished with their questioning, the nurses had insisted that Charlie leave along with the others.

During the questioning, Monique had laid back and listened with amazement to her husband's version of the past few days. His memory of everything was so similar to hers and yet so different. He had told the events as though he were really there, clear up to the end of killing Adam Claiborne. Fortunately, the police had not even questioned the shooting as an act of self-defense. Charlie even accounted for his arrest at the Claiborne estate. He explained that he had gone to see Claiborne to work out a payment plan and didn't have enough money for the cab ride over.

Although Charlie's recollection of the story was very close to Monique's, there were some significant differences. He remembered the conversations between himself and Monique differently. He also recounted that after they had found Wilton, they had gone straight to the Claiborne estate . . . no cathedral, no Father Jacob, and no sin of murder to repent.

When the questioning was put to Monique, she dare not relay the events any differently than her husband. She knew if she had tried, they would think she had lost her mind. For a brief moment, as Monique listened to Charlie's account, she even doubted her own sanity; but she knew what she experienced was real. Adam had said that the events were happening twice. Perhaps Charlie was somehow remembering the first time around.

But why had she been left behind with the painful memory of the truth? It would have been much easier to hate Adam and think of him as a killer rather than as a man with a heart who had sacrificed himself. She felt a tremendous loss at his death, an emptiness she would never be able to express. He had given his life for their own and she was the only one who would ever know. It was a painful thought that even Adam's son would never know the truth. Perhaps one day she would find him and tell him. She would have to. She owed Adam that much.

The patient in the bed next to Monique suddenly shifted and moaned softly. Monique turned toward the curtains, wondering who the woman was and why she was there. She hated hospitals and sighed with relief at the thought of being released the following morning. She could go home. Home. It would be so empty without Wilton.

240

"Papa . . . " she whispered softly. The sadness suddenly clenched down on her chest and she began to weep. Wilton was gone. She would never again kiss his cheeks nor feel his loving embrace.

"Why, God, why?" she whispered, trying desperately to stop the aching. He was the only one Adam had been unable to save. He had slipped through the cracks and fallen prey to the love he held for his family.

* * * * *

"Mama," she heard, at first thinking she had imagined it. Monique wiped her eyes and looked up. Amy was silhouetted in the doorway, dressed in a children's hospital gown.

"Oh," Monique sighed softly, holding out her arms. "Come here, baby." As the toddler cooed toward her a smiling nurse stuck her head inside the door, then gently pulled it shut. Monique lifted her daughter into the bed and wrapped her arms around her. Amy snuggled down beside her and fell fast asleep.

Chapter 33

A cool breeze blew a strand of long hair across Monique's face. She tucked it back under her barrette and continued loosening the soil around a potted plant outside the window. She heard a knock at the front door and quickly pulled her head inside. She grabbed a dish towel from the kitchen table and wiped her hands. As she made her way through the living room she glanced over at Amy who was busy playing on the floor. The knock sounded again but it had been reduced to a tap. "I'll be right there," Monique called out discarding the towel on her way. When she swung open the door, a tall elderly black man stared back at her.

"Excuse me, Ms. Sinclair," he smiled apprehensively. "My name is Soley Johnson. I used to work for Adam Claiborne."

"Yes," she said, her legs suddenly feeling weak. It had been over a year since she had heard Adam's name.

"Well ma'am, I'm the legal guardian of his son, Philip."

Monique looked puzzled. She knew Adam had left behind a widow. The old man saw the confusion in the young woman's eyes. "After Mr. Claiborne's death, the boy's mother took off to Georgia. She took everything but the boy, you see," he explained.

"I'm sorry to hear that," she said. "Mr. Johnson, won't you come inside?"

"No, no," he said. "Thank you. I've actually got the boy

with me and he wants to see you. I tried to explain to him that that may not be such a good idea," he hesitated as if choosing his words carefully. "Seeing all the bad things that have happened and all. But the boy was insistent," he said shaking his head in bewilderment.

"Where is he?" she asked.

"He's downstairs. May I send him up?"

"Of course," Monique said.

"You're very kind, ma'am."

She looked down at the little boy and instantly recognized that he was Adam's son. He was a handsome child with bright eyes and a lovely stance. He was carrying a small paper bag.

"Ms. Sinclair?" he said looking up at her with the most serious of expressions.

"Yes?" Monique's eyes were riveted on the child.

"I'm Philip Claiborne. May I come in?"

"Please."

He sat down on the couch like a perfect gentleman.

"Would you like some lemonade, Philip?" Monique asked.

"No thank you. I just want to talk to you for a few minutes. Is that okay?" His eyes shared the intensity of his father's.

"Well, of course," Monique said sitting in the chair opposite him.

He sat for a moment staring intently at her. She could see that he had something very important to say but wasn't finding the courage to begin.

"That's my daughter, Amy," Monique said.

Philip looked over at the little girl on the floor. "She's very nice," he said. Again there was silence. "Ms. Sinclair . . . "

"Yes?"

He studied his shoes then forced his gaze back up to her. "My dad loved me very much. He told me that the other night

243

when I was sleeping." He looked down at the paper bag in his hands and began fidgeting with the top of it. "But I knew it anyway."

Monique's heart sank. She wanted to rush to the little boy and take him into her arms but she knew it would only make his visit more difficult for him.

He looked back up at her. "Do you ever have dreams?"

Monique smiled. "All the time."

Philip thought about this for awhile. "I see my dad in my dreams but when I wake up he's gone."

"But he'll always be in your heart," she said weakly. Even to herself it sounded like a flimsy consolation.

"Yeah," he said. She knew he had heard it before. "Ms. Sinclair . . . "

"Why don't you call me Monique?" she said.

The boy's face instantly got brighter. "My dad calls you Moon."

Monique felt the blood rush from her face. She couldn't possibly have heard correctly. "What did you just say?"

Philip mouth dropped. "Oh ma'am, I'm sorry. Is that a bad name?"

"No Philip, it's fine," she said standing to her feet. She lifted her hand to her temple. The child couldn't possibly have heard that from his father. Adam didn't learn of the nick name until after he became Charlie.

"Ms. Sinclair," Philip said. "I know you're probably busy so I won't keep you," he said like a true adult. He slowly unraveled the top of the paper bag. "My dad said that you were very nice and that maybe we could be friends."

"When did he tell you this?" she asked.

"In my dreams. I know dreams aren't real but I thought I should meet you anyway," he said. "Just because it was so important to my dad. He said to have Soley bring me here and to give you this. He said he had one when he was a little boy and thought you might like one too."

The boy's small hand reached into the bag and pulled something out. Monique's eyes were centered on the tiny fingers that clutched the object. He slowly loosened his grip, revealing a tiny rabbit's foot in the palm of his hand.

Monique stared at it a moment in disbelief. "A rabbit's foot," she whispered.

"You can keep it," Philip said proudly.

As she gently took it from his small hand tears began to roll down her cheeks.

"Don't cry Ms. Sinclair," Philip said with alarm. "I didn't mean to make you upset."

Monique looked down at the enchanting little boy with his shining eyes. "They're tears of happiness," she said.

"Then you do like the present?"

"Very, very much," she smiled. "Thank you, Philip." She wiped her eyes. "I tell you what. Why don't you go get Soley and bring him up? I'll fix us all a snack and we'll talk some more."

For the first time since his arrival Philip smiled grandly. "Really? You want us to?"

"Absolutely," she said.

"Back in a sec'," he said, and raced from the apartment.

Monique clenched the soft little trinket in her hand and held it close. "He's a beautiful boy, Adam," she whispered. "I'll take care of him, I promise."

She opened a small box on the mantel and lay the trinket inside. She looked into a mirror on the wall and adjusted her hair. "Come on sweetie," she said, swooping Amy up into her arms. "We've got a new family to feed."

245